# A Book of
# Naughty Children

Thirty Short Stories

Granada Publishing Limited
Published in 1970 by Dragon Books
Frogmore, St Albans, Herts AL2 2NF
Reprinted 1972, 1974, 1976

First published by Methuen & Co Ltd 1944
Copyright Enid Blyton 1944
Made and printed in Great Britain by
C. Nicholls & Company Ltd
The Philips Park Press, Manchester
Set in Monotype Times

# A Book of Naughty Children

## Enid Blyton

*Illustrated by Eileen Soper*

Dragon

CHAPTER ONE

# The Two Rough Children

There were once two rough children. Some children have nice manners, and some haven't. Well, Katie and Sam hadn't. How the other children hated them!

Sam was always coming up to them and slapping them so hard on the back that they nearly fell over. And Katie loved to pinch people and pull their hair. Sometimes Sam tickled another boy or girl – and how his hard fingers did hurt! And often Katie slapped people so hard that it made them blink tears away from their eyes.

Now you might think that the other children would soon slap back, and pinch and punch too – but they didn't, because Sam and Katie were so big for their age. The other children were half afraid of them. So they did their best to keep out of their way, but that wasn't much good, you may be sure.

Now one day, to Sam's great surprise and Katie's too, they had an invitation to a party. The card didn't come through the post, but was left on the seat in their garden, which was rather strange. Katie opened the blue envelope and this is what she read:

"The Knockabout Goblins are giving a party on Tuesday night at twelve o'clock in the buttercup-field. Please come."

Well! Sam and Katie stared at one another in delight and surprise. A fairy party! With goblins! Perhaps there would be a dance – and they might even see the Fairy King and Queen! Oooh, what a treat!

"I expect the other children have been asked too," said Sam. But to their great surprise they found that no other child had had an invitation. They were the only ones.

That made the two children feel very proud indeed. "We are the only ones asked!" said Katie, and she felt so pleased that she slapped the girl standing near her.

"Aren't you sorry you're left out?" said Sam, and he

5

punched Alan hard for nothing at all. Those two children simply could *not* keep their big hands to themselves.

Well, the party night came. Sam and Katie went to bed as usual – but they didn't go to sleep, you can imagine! When half-past eleven came, Katie put on her best pink silk party-frock with red ribbons, and Sam put on his silk blouse and brown knicker-bockers. Then they crept out of the house and ran to the buttercup-field.

As soon as they got near they could hear the sounds of a party. Oh, what fun! They heard a drum going "Boom-boom, boom," and fiddles squeaking high, "Eee-eee-eee!" and trumpets sounding loud, "Toot-ti-toot, toot-ti-toot!"

They got to the stile – and what a sight they saw! There were about a hundred goblins in the buttercup-field, all nearly as big as the children, and all racing about like mad, and shouting and jumping. Suddenly they saw the two children and they ran to the stile.

"Here are Sam and Katie! Come on, children! We did hope you would come. We were not allowed to ask any one else but you."

The goblins pulled the children into the field. "Dance with me!" said a fat goblin to Katie, and he held her tightly. Sam was taken round and round by three goblins, in a dance he didn't know at all.

It was a dreadful dance. The thing to do was to bump into every one else at top speed, and then shout with laughter. Then other goblins bumped into *you* and tried to make you fall on the ground. Katie didn't like it. As for poor Sam, he had a very rough time of it with his three goblins, for they swung him round so fast that he got giddy. They bumped him into about fifty others, and then at last they fell to the ground, with Sam underneath.

The music stopped. Katie looked at her pretty party-frock. It was torn and dirty already. What would her mother say? A goblin came up and screeched loudly in her ear. "EEEEEEEE! I'm an engine going through a tunnel. EEEEEEEEE!"

This was the thing that Sam and Katie often did to scare other children – and now Katie was so scared herself that she ran away. But the goblin put out his hand and caught hold of her by her red ribbons – and they came off and tore a hole in her frock. Instead of saying he was sorry, the goblin grinned and tied the ribbons round his own head.

6

"Don't do that!" cried Katie angrily. But the goblin only danced round her and laughed.

Then some one began to shout. "A ring, a ring – make a ring! We're going to play the slapping game!"

So a large ring was made, and Sam and Katie were pushed outside it. "How do we play this game?" asked Sam. "I don't know it."

"Oh, you run round the ring and try to get in somewhere," said the goblin. "And as you pass we can slap you. It's a fine game!"

Well, it may have been a fine game for the goblins, but it wasn't at all nice for Sam and Katie. As they ran round the ring, trying their hardest to squeeze into it, the goblins unlinked their hard, horny hands and slapped the children.

"Slap! Smack! SLAP! Thwack! Slippity-slap!"

Katie began to cry. The slaps hurt. "Don't do that!" she sobbed. "Don't do that!"

Sam got such a hard slap that he lost his temper. He turned on the goblin who had slapped him.

"If you do that again you'll be sorry!" he said. The goblin did it again – "SLAP!" Sam kicked him – and at once a shout went up.

"The kicking game! The kicking game!" Before the children knew what was happening, the goblins had made two long lines, with the children in the middle.

"Go on, Sam – go on, Katie!" cried the top goblin. "Run down the lines as fast as you can. This is the kicking game."

By now the two children wanted to get back home as quickly as they could, so they ran down between the two lines at top-speed – and do you know, as they went those horrible little Knockabout Goblins tried to kick them. Poor Sam and Katie! How bruised and sore they felt!

"I hate this, Katie," said Sam. "Whatever will they do next?"

The next game was something to do with pinching and pulling, and Katie turned quite pale. She was sure that she would be pinched and pulled about, and the goblins were so strong that it really wasn't much good trying to pinch and pull back. But just as the game was about to begin, there came a great silence, and suddenly every goblin fell down on one knee.

The children looked up. A fairy with a beautiful face and long silver wings trailing behind her had just flown down.

7

"The Princess! The Princess Peronel!" cried every one.

"Good evening, goblins," said the Princess in a voice like the twittering of a swallow. "I hope your party is a good one?"

"Find, fine!" cried the goblins.

"And I hope your two guests are enjoying it too?" said Peronel, looking kindly at Sam and Katie. The children were kneeling, like the goblins, for they felt it must be the right thing to do.

Katie burst into tears. "It's a hateful, horrid, nasty party!" she sobbed. "My dress is spoilt and torn. I have been smacked and slapped and kicked, and so has Sam. If I'd known it was to be such a rough party I wouldn't have come."

Princess Peronel looked surprised. "But you love being rough," she said. "I've often watched you in the playground at school, slapping and pushing and pinching and poking. I always let the Knockabout Goblins ask two children to their party, and I thought, as you loved rough things, you would enjoy the party."

Sam and Katie went red. They didn't know what to say.

"You *do* like being rough, don't you?" said Peronel, still looking puzzled.

"Yes," said Katie, wiping her eyes. "I suppose we do – but we don't like it when people are rough to *us*!"

"Oh, but that's not fair!" said Peronnel, suddenly looking stern. "Not fair at all. Do the others like it when you are rough to *them*?"

"No," said Sam. "I see what you mean, Princess. We've been doing what people hate – and we hate it too, when it's done to us. Please let us go home. We've learnt our lesson."

"Well, you may go," said Peronel. "But be careful not to come near the buttercup-field again if you act roughly – because the Knockabout Goblins will love to play with you, you know."

The children got up from their knees and ran home at once, not even looking behind to see what the goblins were doing. And do you suppose they pinch and punch and slap and smack now? My goodness, no! They don't want to play with the Knockabout Goblins again, you may be sure.

## CHAPTER TWO

## Billy Bitten-Nails

Billy Brown had such a funny name at school – he was called Billy Bitten-Nails! I expect you can guess why! He bit his nails very badly, and they looked dreadfully ugly.

His mother asked him not to bite them. His teacher told him how horrid they looked. His friends laughed at him and said his nails must taste nice because he always seemed to be eating them. But nothing that any one said made any difference to Billy Bitten-Nails. He just went on biting them.

Now one day Billy did a good turn to the pixies. He happened to be going through the woods when he heard somebody making such a fuss.

"Look at that!" cried a little high voice. "Right up in the tree, where I can't possibly reach it! It's too bad of the goblins to play a trick like that on me. I can't possibly get it again – it's much too high in the tree!"

Then Billy heard other little voices, and he peeped round the tree to see what all the fuss was about, and to his great surprise he saw three small pixies looking up into a prickly holly tree!

"Hallo!" said Billy. "What's the matter? What is up in the tree?"

"My best hat," said one of the pixies. "The goblins came along a few minutes ago, snatched my hat off my head, and threw it up into the tree. I can't get it because it's too high up, and the tree is terribly prickly."

"Well, I'll get it for you," said Billy, picking up a stone. "I can aim very well. I'll knock your hat out of the tree in a twinkling! Stand away or the stone may hit you."

Billy threw the stone hard at the hat. It hit it – bang! The hat fell down out of the tree, almost on to the waiting pixie's head. He gave a squeak of delight and caught it.

"Thank you, you kind boy!" said the little fellow. "It's so

good of you to help me. I'll do something for you in return. Now, let me look at you – I wonder what you'd like me to do!"

The tiny pixie stared hard at Billy from his head to his feet, and suddenly he saw Billy's bitten nails. He smiled and nodded his gay little head.

"Ah!" he said. "I see you hate your nails! You are trying to bite them all away. I will help you! If you don't want your nails you needn't have any!"

Before Billy could say anything the little pixie touched all his nails one after the other with his own tiny fingers. As he touched them he said such a magic word that Billy trembled. He had never heard a magic word before and it had a very strange and curious sound.

"There you are!" cried the pixie in delight. "You won't have to bite your nails away any more! They are gone!"

Billy looked down at his hands – and how he stared! All his nails were gone! Yes – really. His fingers were very queer-looking indeed – just fingers right to the top without any nails at all. Whatever would every one say?

"Oh, please, I don't like this," he began – and then he stopped. The pixies had vanished! Not a sign of them was to be seen. And there was poor old Billy, with no nails on his fingers. He put his hands into his pockets and walked off home, feeling most alarmed.

He kept his hands in his pockets all that afternoon, and, as Mother was out to tea, he had it alone, and no one noticed how queer his fingers looked as he spread his jam and cut his cake. Poor Billy! He couldn't scratch his knees where his shorts rubbed against them, because he hadn't any nails. He couldn't scrape the earth off his sleeve where he had fallen into the mud, because he hadn't any nails to do it with! He couldn't even open his pocket-knife as usual, because he hadn't even a bitten nail left to open it with!

"This is simply dreadful!" said Billy to himself. "Whatever am I to do? I miss my nails terribly. And how shall I explain at school what has happened?"

Well, you should have seen his mother's face when at last she saw that Billy had no nails! She simply couldn't believe it! And when Billy told her what had happened she grew quite pale.

"Oh dear! I wonder if this means that your nails will never

10

BILLY LOOKED DOWN AT HIS HANDS — AND HOW
HE STARED

11

grow again," she said. "Your fingers do look so horrid, Billy. I can't imagine what your teacher will say."

Well, his teacher said quite a lot, and so did the boys and girls.

"I don't know which is the more horrid of the two, Billy," said his teacher, "to have bitten nails, or to have no nails at all. You are a most unfortunate little boy. First you make your own fingers ugly, and then the pixies make them even uglier! Well, you must do the best you can without nails. You must get the other children to open your pocket-knife for you when you want to sharpen your pencils."

Billy didn't say anything. He wished and wished that he had never in his life bitten his nails! It was very bad luck that just when he had seen and helped the pixies for the first time, the reward they had given him was something he didn't want.

"I'll go through the woods again and call the pixies," thought Billy to himself. "Perhaps they will give me my nails back again."

So he went. He stood beneath the big holly tree and called loudly. "Pixies! Pixies! It is Billy calling you. I want you!"

Up ran the tiny pixie whose hat he had got from the tree. "Hallo, Billy!" he said. "What's the matter?"

"It's my nails," said Billy. "I want them back."

"But why?" asked the pixie in surprise. "You had tried to bite them right away. If you don't like your nails it would be silly to have them again."

"I *do* like my nails," said Billy. "It was a silly habit I got into. Please give them back to me."

"Well," said the pixie, "I can make them begin to grow again, Billy, but I'm afraid they won't be quite the same sort of nails that you had before. If you bite them they will squeal out, because they will be magic nails. You will hurt them if you bite them."

"Well, I won't bite them," said Billy. "Please make them grow again."

The pixie took a small twig growing nearby and touched the tips of Billy's fingers with it, saying another magic word, even stranger than the first he had used. Billy looked at his fingers. He saw that tiny nails were just beginning to grow! Good!

"They will take a few days to get to the tips of your fingers," said the pixie. "I'm sorry I did something you didn't like, Billy. Good-bye!"

12

He disappeared, and Billy went home, feeling very glad to have his nails growing again. It was wonderful to see them grow! In a week's time they were almost at the tips of his fingers! Billy was pleased.

And then, in school one morning, Billy quite forgot and began to nibble the nail on the first finger of his right hand! And what do you suppose happened?

The nail squealed out. Yes, it did really. "Eeeeee!" it squealed. "EEEeeeee!"

Billy was startled. His teacher looked up. "How dare you make that noise, Billy!" she said. "Go into the corner!"

"It was my nail that squealed," said Billy.

"Don't tell me such silly stories," said his teacher. And Billy had to go into the corner.

The next time that Billy bit his nails he was in church on Sunday. Oh dear, oh dear! He bit the nail on the little finger of his left hand – and it squealed out loudly.

"Eeeeee! Ooooo! Eeeee!"

Billy's father was so angry. He took Billy by the arm and marched him straight out of church. Billy didn't dare to tell his father that it was his nail that had squealed, because he felt sure his father wouldn't believe him. He was in disgrace all that day.

The next time that Billy bit his nails he was at a party. It was a most exciting one and Billy began to bite his nails.

"Eeeeee!" said one nail.

"Oooooo!" said another.

"Ow-ow-iw-ow!" said a third.

Every one looked at Billy.

"Poor little boy. He doesn't feel well," said the lady who was giving the party. She took Billy's arm and went out of the room with him. "You had better go home, Billy," she said. "You are not well."

"It was my nails that squealed like that, not me," said poor Billy.

"Oh no, dear," said the lady. "You mustn't tell silly stories like that. Here's your coat. Run home and tell your mother you don't feel well."

Billy went home – and on the way he made up his mind that never, never again would he bite his nails. It was simply dreadful to have them squealing like that! He would let them grow properly, and perhaps in time they would be like every one else's nails.

So he hasn't bitten them again. He showed them to me yesterday. They are so nice and round and long – but I do wonder what will happen when he cuts them? Perhaps they won't mind that – perhaps it is only biting they don't like! What do *you* think?

CHAPTER THREE

## Tom Noddy's Imp

Once upon a time there was a boy who couldn't keep his fingers off anything! He was for ever meddling with other people's things, and sometimes he even took what didn't belong to him!

His mother was angry, and she was sad. But Tom Noddy still went on meddling. If his father left his pincers or his hammer and nails out, Tom Noddy would be sure to spy them and use them. He might pinch his fingers and hammer his thumb, but it didn't teach him not to touch what didn't belong to him!

If his mother went to answer the door-bell when she was making cakes, Tom Noddy would go and meddle with her dishes – emptying the milk into one – and currants into another – so that the cakes were spoilt and his mother was cross.

And at school he was just as bad. He would take some one else's new pencil, and break the point as he tried it. He would borrow a rubber and lose it. He would open some one's nice new paint-box and mix up all the paints with his meddling fingers. Really, Tom Noddy was a perfect nuisance.

Aha! But one day he meddled with the fairy folk – and you can't do that easily. They won't stand it. It happened like this.

Tom Noddy was out one afternoon, peeping into all the hedges to see if he could find any birds' nests. And what should he see but a hole in a tree and green smoke coming out of it!

14

Now Tom Noddy would have run, if he had been wise, for green smoke, as every one knows, is a sure sign there's a witch about! But Tom Noddy wasn't going to run – not he! He wanted to find out what made the green smoke!

So he popped his hand down the hole in the tree and felt about. His fingers touched something that felt like a perfectly round egg. He took it out of the hole and looked at it.

It was a very queer egg – if it was one. It was as round as a ball, bright green with yellow spots, and had six little black holes in it out of which the green smoke came! How curious!

"Hie! Put that back!" called a voice.

Tom Noddy turned round and saw a goblin's face looking at him round a tree. "That belongs to old Witch Needles!" shouted the goblin. "She'll be cross if she finds some one's been meddling with her impy-egg!"

"Impy-egg!" thought Tom Noddy, "oh, this sounds interesting. I'll take the egg home and have a look at it!"

So, turning his back on the goblin, he ran off home, holding the smoking egg in his pocket. But no sooner did he get home than the egg broke! It crumbled to pieces in his pocket, and Tom Noddy shook the bits of shell out, wondering what was inside the egg.

And out of his pocket, with the egg-shell, came a tiny black imp, with eyes as green as grass! The imp leapt on to the table and shouted in a loud voice:

"Ooee, ooee, ooee, oo!"

"Tom Noddy! Stop that noise!" shouted his mother crossly. "Don't you know I'm having a rest. Get off to afternoon school at once."

"Ooee, ooee, ooee, ooee, oo!" yelled the imp. Tom heard his mother leaping off her bed, and he fled – for he knew he would get a whacking if he stayed. His mother would believe no stories about little black imps.

"Ooee, ooee, ooee, oo! Take me with yooee, yooee, yooee, you!" shrieked the imp and jumped straight into Tom's pocket. Tom jogged on to school, not knowing the black impet was there at all!

He was just in time for school. He sat down at his desk, and began his work. The imp crept out of his pocket and began to look about. He was just like Tom – a real little meddler! He slid over to Tom's pencil-box and took out a pencil – a fine sharp one, longer than the imp himself! He pressed on it – and

15

crack! The point broke! The imp leapt back into Tom's pocket in fright, Tom saw his pencil rolling down the desk – then bump, it went on the floor.

"Silence!" said the master.

"Ooee, ooee, ooee, oo!" shrieked the imp, poking his head out of Tom's pocket. Tom jumped – he knew the imp was there, but no one else did. The master thought that Tom Noddy was calling "ooee!" and he was very angry with him.

"Come and stand out here," he said sternly. So Tom had to come and stand by the master's desk. The imp hopped out of his pocket in a moment, and crept on to the desk. He found a pen-nib and crept back again. He pushed the nib into Tom and pricked him.

"Ooooh!" squealed Tom.

"Ooee, ooee, ooee, oo!" squealed the black imp too, in delight.

"Tom Noddy, how dare you behave like this!" cried the master. "Go outside the room."

Poor Tom! He went out and stood there, hoping the head master wouldn't come by. He took the imp out of his pocket and went to a nearby cupboard. He opened the door, popped the imp inside and shut the door firmly. Ha, ha! That would get rid of the imp!

"Ooee, ooee, ooee, oo!" cried the imp, battering the door with his tiny hands.

The head master flung open *his* door and looked down the passage.

"Is it *you*, Tom Noddy, making that terrible noise?" he roared. "There seems to be no one else here."

"Please, sir, it's a little black imp in the cupboard," said Tom. The head master went to the cupboard opened the door and looked in. The tiny imp slipped out without being seen and jumped back to Tom's pocket.

"Ooee, ooee, ooee, oo!" he squealed in delight.

"Go back to your classroom and stay in for an hour after school!" roared the head master crossly. So Tom crept back to his place, wondering whatever the little black imp would do next!

Well, that imp got out of Tom's pocket and wandered all over the classroom, collecting a rubber from this desk, a pencil from that, a nib from a third – and when he had a fine collection he crept back to Tom's desk, under every one's feet.

ALL THE BOYS RACED AFTER HIM

He put them all down very quietly under Tom's desk, and then tried to climb up to Tom's pocket, taking them one by one. It was a difficult job, but that imp managed to do it.

And then every one began to miss what the imp had taken. "My rubber's gone!" said one boy. "My new pen's gone!" said another.

"Ooee, ooee, ooee, oo!" suddenly cried the imp in Tom's pocket. Tom jumped to his feet. "Please, sir!" he cried, "It isn't me – it's a horrid little black imp in my pocket!"

"Oh, really?" said the master. "Well, pray take him out and let us see him, Tom!"

Tom put his hand into his pocket – and brought out every one else's pens, pencils, and rubbers! Oh dear! He stared at them in horror.

"My rubber!" cried a boy.

"My pen!" shouted another.

" And where is this wonderful imp!" said the master. Where indeed? That wicked little imp was crawling all over Tom, tickling him wherever he went – up his back, and down his neck, and down his sleeves – oooh!

"Please, sir, I didn't take all these things," said Tom. "It was that imp."

"I don't believe there is any imp," said the master.

"Ooee, ooee, ooee, oo!" squealed the imp, and he poked his black head out of Tom's coat sleeve!

"There he is, there he is!" cried the boys – and as soon as the imp saw that he was discovered he hopped out of Tom's sleeve, ran over the desk like a big spider, down the leg and over the floor to the door.

"Catch him, catch him!" cried the master.

Every boy jumped out of his desk in delight, and rushed after the imp. He slipped under the door and ran down the passage. All the boys raced after him.

The imp squeezed under the head master's door shouting, "Ooee, ooee, ooee, oo!" at the top of his voice. The head master jumped in fright. Then his door burst open and about twenty boys rushed in.

"What is the meaning of this?" roared the head master angrily. The imp leapt up and jumped into his pocket.

"You've got Tom Noddy's imp, sir!" cried the boys.

"Ooooe, ooee, ooee, oo!" yelled the wicked little black imp, sticking his head out of the pocket. But that was the last time he played his tricks – for the head master got hold of him, held him firmly, took him to the window and threw him out as far as he could.

Splash! He landed in a duck-pond – and was seen no more. Whether a duck ate him thinking he was a fat tadpole, or whether he crawled out and went back to his tree no one ever knew.

But anyway, after that Tom Noddy didn't go meddling with things that weren't his. Not he! He had had enough of little black imps with grass-green eyes.

But whenever any one calls to Tom in the road – "Ooee, ooee, ooee, Tom!" he thinks it is that imp again at first – and he runs like a hare! Poor Tom Noddy!


CHAPTER FOUR

## 'I Shan't'

There was once a silly little girl called Joy. But she wasn't a bit like her name. She made people unhappy, so she ought to have been called Sorrow, not Joy!

She was always saying "I shan't!" I expect you know children like that. They are such a nuisance, aren't they!

When you say, "Let's play snap!" they say, "I shan't!" And when you say, "Let's play Red Indians," they shout, "I shan't!" And they say the same thing to their mothers and nurses.

"Eat up your dinner!" says Mother, and what is the answer she gets? "I shan't!" Well, that was just like Joy. It was always "I shan't, I shan't, I shan't!"

And then one day a speck of magic dust flew into her mouth as she was saying "I shan't!" and twisted up her tongue so that she could only say those two words and no others.

It was just at that moment that Joy's Aunt Dorothy came to see her. She brought with her a lovely box of chocolates, and when she took the lid off, what a fine sight they were!

"Take two of these lovely chocolates, Joy dear," her aunt said, holding out the box.

Joy was going to say thank you – but her tongue could only say two words, "I shan't!"

"Dear me!" said her aunt offended. "Pray don't take any if you don't want to!" And she shut the box up.

"Joy, how rude!" said her mother. "Say you are sorry at once and Auntie will forgive you."

"I shan't!" said Joy's tongue, before she could say anything else.

"You naughty little girl!" said Mother. "Go upstairs at once."

"I shan't!" said Joy's tongue, and she burst into tears. It was dreadful to keep saying "I shan't" when she so badly wanted to be nice to Auntie Dorothy and Mother.

She went upstairs and cried in her bedroom. "I simply must say something else to Auntie," thought the little girl. "I will tell her I am very sorry. Now – I'll open my mouth and say it quickly!"

But as soon as she opened her mouth only two words flew out – "I shan't!"

Soon Mother came up. "Wash your hands and come down-stairs," she said. "It is dinner-time. Hurry up."

"I shan't!" said Joy, though she badly wanted to say something else.

She washed her hands and went downstairs. Auntie had gone. Daddy was at home for dinner and he smiled at Joy.

"Eat up your dinner quickly and we'll go down to the river this afternoon," he said. "You'll like that, Joy."

"I shan't," said Joy's tongue at once.

"Don't talk to *me* like that," said Daddy in a cross voice. "Talk properly and politely."

"I shan't!" said Joy. Wasn't it dreadful? She simply couldn't help it.

"Well, *I* can say 'I shan't' too," said Daddy. "Listen! *I shan't* take you to the river! I *shan't* kiss you good-night!"

"And I can say it too," said Mummy. "I *shan't* let you have cake for tea! I *shan't* take you to see Granny to-morrow. I *shan't* give you any treats at all!"

Joy began to cry again. It was no use explaining to Daddy and Mummy – because all the words she could say were "I shan't!" Wasn't it dreadful for her?

Mummy and Daddy went out after dinner and wouldn't take Joy with them. She was left in the garden to play. She was very miserable. As she lay on the grass a ball came bouncing over the wall. It had come in from the road outside. Two big boys looked over the fence.

"Will you throw us back our ball?" said one.

Joy wanted to say she would – but once more her tongue said "I shan't!" in a very rude voice.

"Horrid girl!" said the boys, and they jumped over the fence to get the ball themselves. One of them pulled Joy's hair hard, and the other pinched her arm.

"Nasty little 'I shan't', aren't you!" said the bigger boy. "You'd better throw our ball back *next* time!"

"I shan't!" said Joy. She simply couldn't say anything else. The boys gave her a slap and jumped back into the road. Joy lay down on the grass again and cried herself to sleep. And whilst she was asleep the magic speck of dust slipped off her tongue and down her throat. So when she woke she found that she could talk properly again. She was *so* glad!

But, you know, she is so afraid of getting her tongue stuck again that she has never said "I shan't" since that day! Her mother can't think why she is so much nicer. It really was a dreadful thing to happen, wasn't it!

CHAPTER FIVE

## *The naughty little story-teller*

There was once a boy called Benjy who was a naughty little story-teller. He just didn't bother to tell the truth when he was asked.

If his mother said to him, "Benjy, is it six o'clock yet, your bedtime?" he would say, "No, Mother, it's only ten to."

And then the clock would strike six, so his mother knew he was telling stories She didn't know what to do with him, and neither did his teacher.

But some one else knew what to do. Just listen!

As Benjy was coming home from school one day, he met an old woman. She said to Benjy, "Good morning, little boy.

Are you going to the village? If you are, take me with you, because I don't know the way."

Now Benjy *was* going to the village, for that was where he lived – but he wasn't going to say so, because he wanted to run home and not walk slowly with an old woman. So he said, "No, I'm not going to the village I'm afraid. But you'll easily find it. It's across this field, and over the stile and down the road and . . ."

"You are a naughty little story-teller, Benjy," said the old woman suddenly, looking at him with wide-open, piercing eyes. "You *are* going to the village! Well, you won't go there this morning, anyhow! Come with me!"

She took hold of his arm and Benjy had to go with her. He was rather frightened. The old woman led him through a hole in the hedge that he had never noticed before, and into a lane that was quite new to him. Down the lane they went to a village that Benjy was most surprised to see – for in it were brownies, gnomes, pixies, witches – and even a big giant, who, however, was full of smiles and not at all frightening.

"You might let me go," said Benjy, pulling at the old woman's arm. "My mother has a chocolate pudding for my dinner to-day, and I'm hungry. She will be cross with me if I'm late."

"Very well then, go!" said the old dame, and she let go of Benjy's hand. He darted away up the lane down which they had come – but somehow it seemed different – and to his surprise he came, before long, to a tumble-down cottage, outside which sat a long-nosed brownie, knitting a red sock.

"Please," said Benjy, "could you tell me the way home? I want to get to Hillside Village."

"Yes, certainly," said the brownie, beaming. He pointed across a field with his knitting-needle. "Just trot across that field and you're there!"

So away trotted Benjy across the field – but dear me, on the other side of the field was a broad river and he couldn't possibly get across. He frowned angrily at the water.

"That horrid brownie told me an untruth!" he said. "I know my home isn't this way."

He saw a little man coming up the river-path and he called him.

"I say! Which is the way to Hillside Village?"

"Catch the bus at the corner!" said the little man, pointing to where a lane turned a corner nearby. Benjy ran to the corner and stood there. He stood there for five minutes. He stood there for ten minutes. He stood there for *twenty* minutes! Still no bus. Then he saw a brownie boy and shouted to him.

"How soon does the bus come along?"

"What bus?" asked the boy in surprise.

"The bus that goes from here to Hillside Village, of course," said Benjy.

"There isn't one," said the boy, grinning. "Some one's been telling you a story!"

Benjy was too angry to speak.

"If you want to get to Hillside Village, you must walk up the hill there, down the other side, across a field where you'll see some geese, and then over the stile in the corner," said the brownie boy. "But it's no good waiting for a bus, because one won't come."

"Thank you," said Benjy and walked off. He climbed the hill, which was very steep. He went down the other side. He came to the field and saw some geese there. He walked into the field – and all the geese chased him with hisses and cackles till he reached the stile in the corner – and there he found a red-faced farmer waiting for him!

"What are you doing in my field?" he roared.

"Nothing," said poor Benjy. "Only just trying to find my way home to Hillside Village."

"Well, you won't find it *this* way," said the farmer angrily. "Disturbing all my geese! I've a good mind to spank you! You've come the wrong way for Hillside Village. You want to go right in the opposite direction. Some one's told you a story if they said come this way!"

"This is a hateful place for telling stories," said Benjy, almost in tears. "Every one tells me stories."

"Dear me, that's strange," said the farmer, looking closely at Benjy. "I wonder why they do. Is it anything to do with yourself, do you think?"

"I don't know what you mean," said Benjy, going red.

"Oh, well, think about it," said the farmer, going off. "I just wondered."

Benjy sat on the stile and thought about it. Could it be that every one was telling him stories because he himself was a story-teller? Had that old woman been punishing him like

"WHAT ARE YOU DOING IN MY FIELD?" HE ROARED

that – making every one behave to him as he had behaved to every one else? How perfectly horrid!

"I don't like it a bit," said Benjy, out loud. "I've walked miles – all for nothing, I've stood ages waiting for a bus that didn't come. I'm hungry as can be, and I know mother will be very cross. Perhaps she won't have saved me any chocolate pudding at all."

"Hallo, Benjy," said a voice. Benjy looked round. He saw the same old woman that he had seen at first.

"How do you like story-tellers?"

"I don't like them at all," said Benjy.

"Neither do I," said the old woman. "They are most unpleasant people, aren't they?"

"Yes," said Benjy, "and I'm going to stop being one now I know what they are like."

"Good," said the old woman. "Well, you can go home now. Get over the stile and you'll know where you are."

Benjy hopped over the stile – and to his great surprise he found that he was just at the end of his road. How strange! He rushed home at once. His mother met him at the door with a frown.

"You're very late, Benjy," she said. "What happened? I suppose you'll tell me some story or other, so I might just as well not ask you."

"I'll tell you the *truth*," said Benjy, and he told his mother everything that had happened. His mother was most astonished. "Well," she said, "I'll believe all this if you *do* turn over a new leaf, Benjy, and never tell stories again!"

Benjy always does tell the truth now – but wasn't it queer how he learnt his lesson!

CHAPTER SIX

## *The magic biscuits*

Cathy and John were skipping home through the woods when they saw a little paper bag lying by a tree.

"Look," said Cathy, stopping. "There's a bag, and it looks as if it's full of something."

"Perhaps some one has dropped it," said John.

"Let's see what's inside," said Cathy. So the children ran to the bag and Cathy picked it up.

"Ooh!" she said, "it's full of biscuits. Look, John!"

"They are letter biscuits!" said John. And so they were. Each little biscuit was made like a letter. There were A's and B's and C's – they were really most exciting little biscuits.

"Aren't they lovely!" said Cathy. "I wonder who they belong to."

"We'd better take them along with us and see if we find any one looking for them," said John.

So Cathy carried the bag – but how she peeped and peeped into it – and how she longed to nibble some of those dear little biscuits!

"I'm so hungry, John," she said. "Do you suppose I might eat just *one* biscuit?"

"Certainly not," said John. "They don't belong to us, Cathy. You know Mother wouldn't like us to do a thing like that."

"But no one would know if I ate one or two," said Cathy.

"You would know yourself," said John. "It's not nice to know you've done something mean."

"Well – I don't care," said Cathy. "I'm just *going* to eat some  Look – here's a C for Cathy "

She took out a letter C – and popped it into her mouth. She crunched it up – it was delicious.

"I think you're naughty," said John. Cathy took no notice. She put her hand into the bag again.

"I shall eat my name," she said. "I've eaten the letter C – now I want A!"

She found an A and ate that too. Really, the biscuits were the very nicest she had ever tasted! John longed to have one too, but he wouldn't. It was bad enough having a sister who took what wasn't hers!

"Now I want the letter T," said Cathy, and she hunted about for a T. "I've had a C and an A; T comes next in my name."

She found a letter T and put it into her mouth. She crunched it up and swallowed it. John walked on crossly.

"Miaow!" suddenly came a voice. "Miaow!"

John looked round in amazement. Where was the cat?

He soon saw it – a big golden-furred cat that ran after him and mewed.

"Cathy, look at this cat!" called John, looking for his sister – but Cathy had disappeared  She just simply wasn't there. Wherever could she have gone? The bag of biscuits lay on the ground – but Cathy was quite gone.

"Miaow, miaow, miaow!" said the golden cat, and purred and rubbed herself against John's legs. John bent down to stroke her – and looked into the cat's eyes. They were as blue as his sister Cathy's!

"Oh dear, oh dear!" said John, in a fright. "Have you turned into a cat, Cathy?"

"Miaow, miaow!" said the cat sadly.

John stared at her. She had fur as golden as Cathy's hair, and eyes as blue as Cathy's. Cathy had certainly changed into a cat! But why?

"It must be those biscuits!" groaned poor John. "They must be magic ones – but why should they turn Cathy into a cat?"

He soon knew! Cathy had wanted to eat her name in the biscuits – and she had got as far as C-a-t – and the magic in the biscuits had worked – and turned her into what C-A-T – spelt! Cat! Whatever was John to do?

"Oh, why did I let Cathy eat those biscuits?" said John. "I knew it was wrong. Cathy, Cathy, you are a lovely golden cat now – but I want you to be my sister, not a cat."

The little boy picked up the bag of biscuits and looked all round. If only he could find out who they belonged to! Perhaps the owner would help him, and turn Cathy back to her right shape again. He walked on between the trees and at last came to a small yellow cottage that he was sure he had never seen before. With the cat at his heels he walked up the path and knocked at the door.

"Come in!" called a voice. John opened the door and looked inside. He saw a bent old gnome there, stirring something in a big black pot over the fire.

"Good morning," said John.

"Morning," said the gnome, turning round and blinking at John. "What do you want? Are you selling anything?"

"No," said John. "I just wondered if you knew who these biscuits belonged to."

"Of course I don't," said the gnome, who didn't seem to be

in a very good temper. "I like the look of that cat of yours, though – beautiful creature, she is! I'll buy her from you!"

"Oh, no," said John, alarmed. "You can't have her. She belongs to me."

"Here's a piece of gold for her," said the gnome, and pushed a large piece of gold into John's hand. "Go on your way now. The cat is mine!"

And, to John's horror, the gnome pushed him out of the cottage and slammed the door in his face. The cat was left behind in the house! Poor Cathy!

"Miaow! Miaow!" she cried, and tried to get out – but the door and the window were both shut.

John banged at the door – but it was locked. He couldn't think *what* to do. He still had the bag of biscuits in his hand. If only he could find the owner and get some help! The little boy wandered off again, hoping he would meet some one.

And at last he did. He met an old, old woman, bent double under a pile of sticks which she was taking home for firewood. She had a red face and twinkling eyes, and she looked so kind that John ran to ask her help.

"Do you know any one who has dropped a bag of biscuits?" he asked.

The old woman shook her head. "Could you help me with this bundle of wood?" she said. "You look a strong boy. I'll carry the biscuits for you."

So John took the wood from her and walked beside her until they came to a tiny house under a tree – so tiny that John really wondered if there could be room inside to live!

The old woman took the wood and thanked John. "Why do you look so miserable?" she asked. "You look as if you've *lost* some biscuits – not found some!"

"I think they must be magic biscuits," said John, and he showed her them. "They have turned my sister into a cat!"

"Stars and moon!" said the old dame, in surprise. "Did they really? Let me have a look at these wonderful biscuits. Yes – they are magic all right. I can tell by the smell of them."

"You see, my sister was eating her name in the letters – her name's Cathy – and she got as far as C-A-T and she turned into a big golden cat," said John. "I don't know what to do about it now, because an old gnome in a cottage gave me a piece of gold for her, and kept her. He pushed me out of the cottage and I had to leave Cathy behind."

28

"He had no right to do that!" said the old woman. "I know him – mean old thing he is, too! Now let me think a bit, little boy. I'm not a witch or anybody very clever – but I've lived among fairy folk all my life and know their ways."

She sat down on the low wall outside her tiny house and looked at the biscuits.

"So, Cathy turned into a cat because she ate C-A-T!" she said. "Well, little boy, listen – suppose you creep back to the cottage and give the cat two more letters – H and Y, to finish her name. Perhaps she will change back to Cathy then! What a shock for the gnome!"

"Ooh! That's a good idea!" said John, pleased. "I didn't think of that! I'll go back to the cottage at once, and see if I can give Cathy the other two biscuits to finish her name!"

So off he went back to the gnome's cottage. The window was now the smallest bit open at the bottom. John peeped in. The gnome was drying his hands on a towel at the other end of the kitchen. Cathy was lying down on a mat, mewing.

"Cathy!" whispered John. "Eat these two biscuits, quickly – the H first and then the Y. Hurry!"

The big golden cat ran up to the window. John dropped two letter biscuits inside – an H and a Y. Cathy pounced on them and chewed them up.

And, no sooner had she eaten them than she shot up into a little girl again There she was, the same golden-haired, blue-eyed Cathy, *so* pleased to be herself again.

The gnome turned round and saw her. He *was* surprised. "What are *you* doing here in my cottage!" he cried. "Go out at once!"

That was just what Cathy was longing to do! She ran to the door, unlocked it, and raced down the path to John. How glad she was to be with him again!

"Quick! Let's go home!" she said. They ran quickly through the wood, found the right path and raced home at top speed.

"Mother! Mother!" cried John, "where are you? We've had such an adventure! Cathy got turned into a cat. She ate some magic biscuits."

They told Mother all about it – and Mother was most astonished. "Let me see these magic biscuits," she said. "This is a wonderful story."

But John hadn't got them! He had left them behind in the

wood. Wasn't it a pity? And when he went to find them the next day they had gone.

"I expect the right owner found them," he said to Cathy. "I wonder if he'll notice that five of the biscuits are gone."

"I shan't do a thing like that again," said Cathy. "It was horrid, being a cat! But it was nice having a tail to wave about, John."

"I don't want you to be a cat again," said John.

I don't expect Cathy ever will be, do you?

## CHAPTER SEVEN

## A little thing that made a big thing

John had a ball. It was a fine ball, because it could bounce higher than John himself, and it was bright red and green. Wherever John went, that ball went too.

"I don't think you had better take the ball out into the street with you," his mother said. "I don't like to see children playing ball in the street. Sooner or later the ball always goes into the road, and that makes motorists very nervous indeed."

"All right, Mother," said John. But he didn't do what he was told. Instead of leaving the ball at home, he put it into his pocket when he went to tea with his Auntie Sue. He was late when he went, so he ran all the way, and didn't play with his ball. But he had plenty of time when he was on his way back. He took out his precious ball and bounced it.

My goodness me, how that ball did bounce! John bounced it harder than ever, just to see how high it really *would* bounce. It flew above his head, and then fell. John put out his hand to catch it.

But he missed the ball, and it fell to the ground, on to the pavement. John was at the top of the hill that led down to the town, so the ball began rolling. John sprang after it. His foot touched it and it shot out into the road.

John ran after it. Did he look and see if anything was coming? No! Children hardly ever do when they play with a ball in the street. They see the ball and nothing else! John was just like that. He darted after his ball.

There was the screech of brakes being put on hard, and every one looked round. John was scared at the noise, remembered that he was in the road, and hopped back quickly to the pavement, where he was safe. He looked to see what had made the noise.

A car had been coming along over the top of the hill at a fast speed. It had suddenly seen John rushing out and had put on its brakes very suddenly, making the screeching noise that every one had heard.

It swung to the other side of the road to avoid John, and crashed into a barrow of apples, being wheeled by Mr. Pip, the apple-man. The barrow was smashed. Mr. Pip jumped to safety. Hundreds of apples were spilt and went rolling down the street!

The milkman was coming up the hill, driving his horse. When the horse heard the crash of the car going into the apple-barrow, it was frightened. It reared up, swung right round, and galloped off at top speed down the hill!

The milkman fell out. He got up at once, and yelled after his horse.

"Hie there! Hie! Come back! Whoa, whoa!"

But the frightened horse took no notice. It galloped down the hill, going faster and faster.

"Runaway horse, runaway horse!" shouted every one. The milk-cart bumped against the kerb, and about fifty bottles of milk jumped out, flew through the air and landed with a crash. Creamy milk began to pour down the hill in a steady stream. The grocer's cat was delighted, and went to lick up what she could.

The horse galloped on. He was on the wrong side of the road, and he knocked over a man on a bicycle. The bicycle had its front wheel badly bent, and the man could not ride it any more. But still the horse went on.

Down at the bottom of the hill was the river. A bridge went over it. The horse galloped towards the bridge, its cart swaying behind it. A car suddenly came over the bridge from the opposite side, and the driver looked in horror at the galloping horse.

What would happen? Would the horse crash into the car,

IT SWUNG TO THE OTHER SIDE OF THE ROAD TO
AVOID JOHN

and kill itself? Would the driver be killed? No one knew. Every one stood and watched in fear.

The driver of the car twisted the steering-wheel round as sharply as he could. He could not stop his car at once because he was going too fast. The car ran over the pavement, crashed through the bridge railings, and fell with a terrific splash into the river below!

"Get the driver out! He'll be drowned!" every one cried. By now the galloping horse had been stopped by a big policeman, who tied it to a post and then ran to help the man in the car.

John had watched everything in the greatest horror. He ran down the hill after the milk-cart. He saw the man being knocked off his bicycle. He saw the car swerve and fall into the river. He knew that car. Yes – John knew that car quite well!

"It's my Daddy's car!" he thought, and he felt suddenly sick. "It's Daddy in that car! He's fallen into the river. He'll be drowned. Oh, Daddy, Daddy!"

He saw his father taken out of the sinking car. He watched him laid on the banks of the river, whilst men tried to bring him to life again. John cried so bitterly that he could hardly see at all.

His father opened his eyes at last. John flung himself on the wet, cold man. "Daddy! I was afraid you'd be drowned. Oh, Daddy, it was all my fault!"

"Silly boy! It was the milk horse's fault!" said somebody.

"It wasn't, it wasn't!" sobbed John. "It was me and my ball. My ball ran into the road. I ran after it. A car swerved away from me and ran into the apple-man's barrow. The crash it made frightened the milkman's horse, and it ran away. And that galloping horse met you and made you fall into the river with your car."

Poor John. Everything he said was true wasn't it? His father talked to him very gravely that night.

"I must pay the apple-man for his lost apples and broken barrow," he said. "I must pay the milk-man for his spilt milk and smashed bottles. I must pay for the cyclist's wheel to be mended. I must pay a great deal of money to get my poor spoilt car out of the river. John, John, you have a very big lesson to learn. A little thing may be a very little thing – but it may cause a very much bigger thing. See what running into the road after your ball has done!"

"I wish it could be put into a story for other children," said John, "then they will know it too!"

So it has, and you've just read it!

## CHAPTER EIGHT

## The greedy little girl

Once upon a time there was a little girl called Janet. She was rather fat – and that was because she really was very greedy!

She always took more cakes than any one else. She always ate the last cake or biscuit off a plate without saying "Does any one want this, please?" She always wanted three helpings of pudding, and how she grumbled if they were not big helpings!

You should have seen her when she went out to a party! Once she ate a whole jelly herself! And she ate six cream cakes once, and five ices. People looked at her and said, "Look! That's Janet! Did you ever see such a greedy child?"

Janet's mother was rather foolish, because she only said, "Oh, Janet, don't be greedy!" instead of seeing that Janet wasn't. And goodness knows what would have happened to the little girl if she hadn't gone to a pixie party.

I'll tell you about it. Janet was running home across the fields when she tripped over a stone. She fell down and rolled into the hedge. Just as she was getting up, she saw a very strange thing. A little door had been opened in a tree just by her, and a small man looked out. He said, "Dear me! What a noise! Who is it, please?"

Then, when he saw it was Janet, he shut the door in a hurry and disappeared. Janet was so surprised that she sat and looked at the tree in the greatest amazement. A fairy in a tree! She had never seen one before.

She jumped up and went to the tree. She found a tiny handle and turned it. The door opened! Janet looked into the tree. There was a flight of steps going downwards. Oooh!

She squeezed herself through the little door, and went down the steps, her heart beating in excitement. She came to a door at the bottom. She opened it.

"Oh!" she said. "A party!"

She was looking into the gayest little room imaginable. It was hung with paper chains and bells and lanterns, and down the middle was a long table with a silver cloth on. Pixies, fairies, and elves were hurrying in, carrying dishes of cakes, jellies, blancmanges, trifles, fruit, buns, sweets – dear me, what a feast! Janet looked and looked – and made up her mind that she was going to that party!

"Hallo!" she said, walking into the room, much to every one's surprise. "I've come to the party too!"

The little folk were too polite to say she couldn't. They found her a chair towards the middle of the table, and Janet sat down. Oh, those pink jellies! Oh, those chocolate cakes! And dear me, could that really be a treacle pudding? It was the first time Janet had seen one at a party, but she thought it was a very good idea.

She didn't wait for the others to begin. She reached out for a chocolate cake and began. How good it was! She took another. Every one round her was now eating and chattering away merrily. But Janet didn't talk. No, she ate – and ate! The other pixies helped themselves to the delicious chocolate cakes too, and soon there was only one left on the plate. Janet hurried up with her last mouthful and reached out for it.

"You didn't ask if any one else wanted it!" said the pixie next to her. "Don't you know that you should bring your manners with you when you come to a party?"

Janet didn't answer. She had seen a green jelly! Oh, she must have some of that! She helped herself – and do you know, she took some hot treacle pudding too, on the same plate! Of course, it melted the jelly, so Janet took some more.

Then she had four ices, one after another. By this time she felt as if she was getting very squashed on her chair. So she dug her elbows into the pixies next to her and said, "Don't come so close to me. You are squashing me!"

The pixies looked at her.

"*You* are squashing *us*!" they said. "Look at yourself!"

Janet looked at herself – and oh dear me, how dreadful – she had grown almost as fat as an air-balloon!

"Fairy food doesn't agree with greedy people," said a pixie

35

across the table, with a grin. 'It blows them up like a balloon! You do look awful!"

Janet was frightened. She stopped eating at once, and sat still, hoping she would get thinner. Soon the pixies and fairies stopped eating and jumped down. They cleared away the dishes and put the table aside. They were going to have games.

But they wouldn't let Janet play. "No," they said, "you are too fat to run. You would spoil everything. We don't like you. Go away! Go and fetch your good manners! Go home and hide yourself under the bedclothes! You are ugly."

Janet began to cry. The little folk laughed at her and the little girl thought she would go home to her mother. She ran out of the room and climbed the steps to the small door that led out of the tree.

But goodness, gracious me – she couldn't get out of the door! She was *much* too fat! No matter how she tried she couldn't get out! How very dreadful! She couldn't stay in the tree all her life long.

Janet cried big tears all down her face. A gnome came by and heard her. He stared in astonishment at the fat little girl trying to get out of the tree.

"You'll never get out of that little door!" he said. "How did you get in?"

"I was thinner when I got in," said Janet, going red.

"You've been greedy, I should think," said the gnome, grinning. "What a fine punishment for you!"

"Could you help me?" asked Janet. "I will do anything for you in return if you really will help me."

"Give me that necklace you are wearing and I'll get you out," said the gnome.

"But it's my nicest one," said Janet, beginning to cry again.

"All right, I won't help you then," said the gnome. But, just as he was running off, Janet called to him. She undid the necklace and threw it to him.

"Please help me," she said.

The gnome fetched a saw, and began to saw the doorway bigger. Janet stood inside the tree and watched him. At last the doorway was big enough for her to squeeze through. She thanked the gnome and ran home as quickly as she could, feeling very fat and heavy.

She ran up the stairs and put herself to bed. She really couldn't bear any one to see her – and do you know, by the time she got up the next morning she had gone down to her right size again! Wasn't that lucky?

Her mother can't think why Janet has stopped being greedy, because the little girl didn't tell any one about the pixie party – but we know why, don't we!

## CHAPTER NINE

## The boy who changed himself

There was once a boy called John who was unkind to his mother. This sounds dreadful, but it was perfectly true.

John was rude and he was unkind. He was not rude or unkind to any one else, and he was always careful to be polite and kind to his father.

He had a nice mother. She had a kind face, and she loved John dearly. She gave him nice food to eat and bought him lovely toys. But if she asked John to run to the post for her, or to go and fetch something, he never would!

"Don't bother me, Mother!" he would say. "I'm busy!"

And if his mother did not give him the pudding he liked at dinner-time he would push away his plate and say rudely, "I won't have this pudding. I don't like it!"

Once, when he was reading, his mother said, "Sit up, John, dear! Your back is all crooked!"

And John said, "Be quiet! I'm reading!"

Would you suppose any child could talk like that to his own mother? Well, John did!

Now one night a very strange thing happened. The moon shone into John's room and he lay looking up at it – and then, to his great astonishment, he saw some small men walking solemnly down the silver moonbeams, right into his bedroom! They had long beards reaching to their toes and grave blue eyes and stern mouths. John sat up in bed and stared.

"Good evening," said the men politely. "Will you come with us? You are wanted by the Chooser."

TO HIS ASTONISHMENT HE SAW SOME SMALL MEN
WALKING DOWN THE MOONBEAMS

"Who is the Chooser?" said John, puzzled. He got out of bed and put on his dressing-gown. This was an adventure!

"You will see," said the little men, and they took John up the moonbeams. They were slippery to walk on, but quite firm. John walked on for a long way and then, to his surprise, came to a little dark house balanced some way up the moonbeams. It had wings, and had flown there, for it still kept flapping them and the strange house swayed a little. Some one opened the door, and John and the bearded men went inside.

The room inside was perfectly round. In the middle was a small table and at it sat the Chooser. He was an old man, very wrinkled, very wise, very stern. He had before him an enormous book, in which he was writing names with a great quill pen.

"Here is John, Your Excellency," said one of the bearded men. The Chooser looked at John. He had queer eyes. They saw right down into John's mind and thought his thoughts!

"Well, John," said the Chooser, turning over the pages of his big book until he came to the letter J's. "I've brought you here to change you to some one else. I hear that you don't like your mother, so I thought I'd let some one else be her boy, and you can go into a home where there is no mother. I don't like to see mothers wasted."

"Mine isn't wasted," said John, alarmed.

"Oh, yes, she is," said the Chooser, taking up his pen and looking for John's name in the book. "Any mother is wasted if she can't get her children to love her."

"But I *do* love her!" said John, surprised.

"No, Your Excellency, he doesn't," said one of the bearded men. "He wouldn't fetch her a handkerchief yesterday."

"And he grumbled because she wanted him to shut the door on Thursday," said another.

"And he was rude to her six times to-day," said a third. "I heard him."

"And last week, when his mother said he must put on his scarf because it was cold, he told his mother she was silly, and when she said he *must* put on his scarf he rushed out, slammed the door and shouted, 'I hate you!'" said the first little man.

"Ah, yes, he certainly doesn't want a mother," said the Chooser. "I'm sorry I chose him to be her boy now. I'll choose some one who wants a kind mother and hasn't got one.

Now here's a girl called Joan – longing to be loved. . . ."

"I *do* want my mother!" said John, almost in tears. "I didn't really mean I hated her. I only just said it."

"But he didn't say he was sorry afterwards, Your Excellency," said one of the men. "So she thought perhaps he meant it. She was very sad that night. She cried a lot!"

"This is very serious," said the Chooser, looking at John. "When mothers cry there is something very wrong. It is plain that a mother is wasted on you. I will choose a new home for you to-morrow!"

"Oh, please don't!" begged John. "My mother loves me, although I am horrid – she does really. You would make her unhappy if you changed me."

"Mothers are queer people," said the Chooser, shaking his head. "No, John, you must be changed. I won't have your mother wasted – such a nice one, too!"

"You needn't change me!" said John suddenly. "I'll change myself! Give me another chance, Mr. Chooser. I'll change myself so that I'm quite a different boy. I couldn't bear to lose my mother!"

"Very well," said the Chooser, shutting his book. "See if you can change yourself. If you can't, I'll send for you again, and change you for some one else. Take him away, please."

The bearded men took John out of the house. They sat him on the slanting moonbeams and gave him a push. He slid all the way down and landed on his own bed – bump! How queer!

"To-morrow I begin to change myself!" said John. "Telling me I don't love my mother indeed! Of course I do! I'll show that Chooser something!"

Well, he did! He gave his mother a hug first thing in the morning to start the day off! He looked at her kind face and thought how he would make her smile that day! Love his mother, indeed! Of course he did!

I couldn't tell you the times John ran errands for his surprised mother that day! I couldn't tell you the number of hugs he gave her! I couldn't tell you how astonished – and delighted – she was! She simply couldn't believe it!

"Why, I do believe you love me, John!" she said at the end of the day.

"Course I do!" said John. "You're the nicest mother in the world! I always knew that even when I was horrid to you!"

Well, that was last week – and John is still being kind and

40

loving! Do you suppose it will last? I hope so, because it would be dreadful if he lost his mother after all, wouldn't it! Mind you keep yours safely!

## CHAPTER TEN

## *The silly-billy*

Billy was a farmer's boy. He was supposed to help in the farm work, but oh, dear me, the things he did! He never used his brains, and he was always muddling things. He looked for hens' eggs in the pigsties, and twice he tried to saddle a cow, thinking he had caught the horse.

So it was no wonder that every one called him Silly-Billy, was it?

One day he left the farmyard gate open, instead of shutting it. The farmer's wife was baking in the kitchen, so busy that she didn't notice Billy had left the gate open. She ran to the scullery to fetch something – and whilst she was there, what do you suppose happened?

Why, the cows wandered out of the gate and came up to the kitchen door. They smelt the fine smell of baking cakes, and one by one they walked into the kitchen. The pig saw them and thought he would go, too, and see what was happening, and three or four hens, always on the look-out for any titbit, hurried through the kitchen door as well!

So when the farmer's wife came running back into her kitchen, what did she see but five red and white cows, the grunting pig, and four hens, all sniffing round to see what they could find!

"Oh, that Silly-Billy!" she cried, as she shooed the animals out of her nice clean kitchen. "If he hasn't left that gate open again! I'll tell the farmer, so I will!"

So when her husband came in for his dinner she told him about Billy and how he had left the farm gate open so that her kitchen had been full of cows, the pig, and the hens.

The farmer was angry.

"That boy doesn't use his brains," he said. "He doesn't think at all! I won't keep him any more, unless he thinks a bit. Hey, Billy, Billy, come here!"

Silly-Billy went running to see what the farmer wanted.

"Now, you look here, Silly-Billy," said the farmer. "You aren't using your brains. If you don't think a bit more about things, you can go home to your Ma. See?"

"Oh, don't send me home," begged Silly-Billy. "Ma would whip me."

"Well, you see you think hard then," said the farmer.

So Billy frowned all day long and really tried to think hard. He noticed that the cat always liked to go into the barn at night to hunt for the mice there. Sometimes the door was shut and she couldn't get in. Silly-Billy thought a lot about that – and he cut a neat little hole at the bottom of the door so that Puss could get in and out as she liked.

The farmer was pleased. "My, Billy, you're using your brains at last!" he said. "It's true you are! Just look at that – a nice big hole cut in the door for Puss to get in and out and catch all the mice. Good boy!"

Silly-Billy was so delighted. He watched the cat getting in and out – and then he remembered that she had four little kittens too. Why shouldn't they all catch the mice?

So Silly-Billy set to work and cut four tiny holes in the door at the bottom, just beside the one big hole he had cut for Puss. The door looked a bit queer when he had finished.

The farmer looked at the four new holes in astonishment. "My, Billy!" he said, "what have you done that for?"

"Why, sir, it's for the four little kittens," said Billy proudly.

"But why do you want to go and cut holes for *them*?" asked the farmer, puzzled.

"So's they can go in and out to catch the mice too," said Billy. "I've cut the holes small to fit them, you see."

"Silly-Billy," said the farmer, and he laughed loudly. "Can't the little kittens use the mother's big hole? Of course they can! They don't want little holes – they can all follow their mother in at the big one, can't they? Now you've spoilt the door."

Billy was sad about that. After all, he really *had* tried to use his brains! He saw that the kittens did use their mother's hole, because they rapidly grew too big for the tiny holes. It was a pity, Silly-Billy thought.

Now one day the farmer called Billy and said he was going to market. It was a windy day and the farmer's two windmills worked round and round in the breeze. The farmer was pleased, for his corn would soon be ground.

"I'm off to market, Billy," he said. "Just keep an eye on the windmills to-day. They'll work well in this wind. You pop in and out of the mills to see things are all right."

"Yes, master," said Billy, pleased.

Now, not long after the farmer had gone to market the wind dropped. Hardly a breeze blew, and the sails of the windmills slowed down and stood still. There would be no corn ground if the wind did not blow to turn the machinery inside the mills!

The wind blew just a little – but not much. The sails of the windmills creaked, but did not go round. Billy was upset. What could he do?

"There isn't enough wind for two windmills, that's what it is!" said Silly-Billy to himself. "I know what I'll do. I'll take off the sails of the other windmill, and that will leave all the wind for the first one. Then its sails will go round nicely."

So the silly boy undid the sails of one windmill. It took him all the afternoon, for it was a difficult job. Still, he was very pleased with himself.

When the farmer came back, he stared in astonishment at his windmills. One had its sails on, and was standing quite still, for there was only a little wind – and the other windmill had no sails at all!

"What is the meaning of this, Billy?" he shouted.

"Oh, sir," said Billy, beaming all over his face, "the wind died down after you'd gone – and there seemed to be only enough for one windmill – so I took the sails off the other, you see – to leave all the wind for the first one!"

"Well, well, well!" said the farmer, staring at Billy. "If the wind's strong enough to blow one, it's strong enough to blow two, my boy – and if there's not enough wind for two there's not enough for one! You stop using your brains now, Billy. I think you can get on better if you don't use them, after all!"

So Silly-Billy doesn't bother to think about things now, and he is quite happy, even if he does sometimes give the pigs duck-food and tries to shell the beans instead of the peas! Poor Silly-Billy – he's a funny one!

## CHAPTER ELEVEN

## Miss waddle-toes

Once upon a time there was a little girl called Anna. She was a dear, pretty little girl – except when she walked! And dear me, when she walked, *how* she turned in her toes!

"I shall call you Miss Waddle-Toes," said Mother. "You walk like a duck, Anna. It looks dreadful. Do turn your feet out, not in!"

But Anna wouldn't bother to remember to turn out her toes properly. She turned them in as much as ever, and only laughed when Mother called her Miss Waddle-Toes.

Now one day Anna had a great surprise. She found a tiny fairy caught in a spider's web, crying loudly for help. The little girl tore the web, frightened away the big spider there, and set the small fairy on the ground.

"You are very kind," said the fairy gratefully. "What can I do for you in return?"

Anna was excited.

"Please," she said, "I have always wanted to go to a fairy party. Do you think I could?"

"Yes," said the fairy at once. "There is a dance to-night under the big oak-tree in the wood over there. But it's fancy dress."

"Oh dear!" said Anna. "I haven't a fancy dress, I'm afraid."

"Well, come anyhow," said the fairy. "We can dress you up somehow, I expect!"

So Anna ran home, feeling so excited that Mother really could *not* think what was the matter with her!

That night, when the moon rose high in the starry sky, Anna slipped out of bed and ran to the window. Yes – it must be time to go to the party, because she could see tiny lights gleaming here and there in the wood. Oh, what fun!

The little girl slipped on her dressing-gown, ran downstairs, let herself quietly out of the garden door, and went down the garden. She slipped through the gate that led into the field, and ran over to the wood.

The party had begun! The wood was lighted with tiny lanterns, and hundreds of pixies, elves, brownies, and gnomes were there, all in fancy dress, talking in high twittering voices, and dancing round and round with each other.

"Hallo!" cried a voice, and a gnome danced up to her. "Here comes Miss Twaddle-Toes, with her toes turned in as usual! Have you come to the party?"

"Yes," said Anna. "The fairy I saved from a spider to-day said I could come."

"Well, you must have a fancy dress," said the gnome, "and you must be made smaller, or you won't be able to dance with us. Wait till I get my wand, then I'll give you some kind of fancy dress."

He ran off and fetched a tiny silver wand with a glittering star on the end. He looked at Anna.

"I don't know what sort of fancy dress will come when I touch you with my wand," he said. "You don't mind, do you?"

"Not at all," said Anna, hoping very much she would have a fairy's dress or perhaps a brownie's suit. "I *should* like something with wings, though."

"Right!" said the gnome. He waved his wand, said a word three times – a very magic one – and touched Anna lightly on the hair, crying, "Change, Miss Waddle-Toes, change! Wear your fancy dress till daybreak!"

Anna felt something funny happening to herself. She was certainly changing. She looked down at herself – and what a dreadful shock she got!

What do you suppose she had changed into? Why, a large yellow duckling with a pair of little flappy wings!

"Quack!" cried Anna in dismay. "Quack!"

"Goodness! She's changed into a duck!" shouted the gnome – and a lot more of the little folk came running up. "Look at that!"

"Well, she shouldn't turn her feet in!" said an elf wisely. "She might have known she'd wear a duck's dress for fancy dress, if she waddled about like one! I've often seen her turning in her toes – dreadful! Never mind, Anna! You are small enough to join us and enjoy the party now."

"Quack, quack, quack!" said poor Anna, who felt she would not enjoy the party at all! She could only quack, not talk, and she waddled along turning in her toes all the time, and couldn't dance a bit! She couldn't even fly, for her wings were really much too small. It was all most disappointing!

"How I wish I had never turned my feet in!" she thought to herself, as she tried to dance with a small fairy in butterfly's dress. "Oh dear – my feet are so big that I keep tramping on this dear little fairy's toes!" She tried to say she was sorry, but all she could say was "Quack, quack, quack!"

However, the fairy understood. "Don't mention it," she said politely, and on they danced.

The party would have been simply lovely, but Anna couldn't even eat or drink, because she didn't know how to manage her big beak! It seemed to get in the way so! In fact, it got in her way just as much as her feet did!

"This is a horrid party after all," thought the disappointed little girl. "I can't dance properly – I can't fly – I can't eat this lovely jelly – I can't drink that lovely pink lemonade – and I've never had *pink* lemonade before! I wish I'd never come!"

She sat down on the grass and watched the others dancing. It was a pretty sight – but Anna was sad. She hated being a duckling. It was horrid to waddle about in a clumsy manner when everyone else was dancing so lightly on tiptoe.

"I'll never turn my toes in again, that's certain!" thought Anna. "I didn't know how clumsy it was till I wore this duck fancy dress and was turned into a duck. I won't be so silly again."

When dawn came the fairy folk fled – and Anna was left sitting on the grass alone. She was upset. Suppose she stayed a duckling! Whatever would Mother say?

She waddled back home and walked up the stairs. She did not dare to call Mother, because she knew she would quack. She got into bed, pulled up the clothes with two little arm-wings, and then fell asleep.

And in the morning she was herself again! Yes, really – she had her own feet and arms and everything – she was a little girl and not a duckling. How glad she was!

She jumped out of bed and dressed. Then she ran to tell Mother her adventure, and dear me – how nicely she turned her toes out as she ran! No more Miss Waddle-Toes for her!

Mother was sorry she had had such a horrid time at the party. "Never mind," she said, "perhaps next time it will be

"QUACK!" CRIED ANNA IN DISMAY. "QUACK!"

nicer – especially if you remember not to walk like a duck any more, Anna! Try hard and see if you can walk like a pixie does!"

Anna *is* trying hard – and if you know any little Miss Waddle-Toes just tell them what happened to Anna. They will soon stop turning in their toes, won't they?

CHAPTER TWELVE

## *Boastful Bill*

Bill was a big boy. He was only eight years old, but he was tall for his age, and every one thought he was ten. He liked people to think that. He boasted that he could do this, that, and the other – he could ride ten miles straight off on his bicycle and not feel tired – he could swim eight times up and down the school baths – he could row a boat across the river and back and not stop once. Oh, Bill was a wonderful chap – if you listened to him!

Next door to Bill lived the twins, Mollie and John. They were seven years old and small for their age. They had no bicycles, so when Bill boasted about his riding, they thought him very wonderful indeed. They had never been in a boat, so they couldn't row. How marvellous Bill must be to row across the river all by himself!

"All the same, I don't much like Bill, although he's so clever and wonderful," said Mollie to John. "He never seems to think any one else can do anything. I know we are small for our age and can't do anything much, but I do get a bit tired of hearing all the things Bill can do!"

When the summer holidays came Bill asked John and Mollie where they were going.

"We are going to Seasands," said Mollie.

"How funny! So am I!" said Bill. "My word, we shall be able to have some fine times together. We have a boat – and a hut – and a floating bed that you blow up and lie on. Last year I had great fun on that – can't tell you how many people I pushed off it into the water! My word, they did swallow a lot of salty water too!"

Mollie and John looked at one another. It wouldn't be much fun to be pushed off the floating bed too often. They were so small, and Bill was so big! Bill could push them off each time, but they were quite sure they wouldn't be able to push him off at all!

The seaside holidays came at last. Mollie and John went down to Seasands with their father and mother. They were so excited about it!

The first person they saw on the beach when they got there was Bill, of course. There he was, sitting in a boat, looking as if the whole place belonged to him.

"Hallo!" he said. "I've just been for a row all round the bay."

Mollie looked at the boat. It seemed very dry outside, not at all as if it had been in the water. But she was too polite to say anything.

"I've bathed twice already to-day," said Bill. "The water was jolly cold, too! I didn't feel warm till I'd swum right out to that rock over there!"

Molly and John looked at the rock. It seemed very far away indeed. They thought Bill must be a fine swimmer to swim so far.

"We can swim too," said John. "But not so far as that."

"Pooh! Little shrimps like you can't do much," said Bill. "I say! What about building a whopping big castle, the biggest ever made? We've plenty of time before the tide comes in. We'll have towers on it and a tunnel right through – and bits of glass from the beach for the windows!"

So they began to build the big castle. Mollie and John worked hard, but Bill didn't seem to do much except tell them how to make the towers and pat the sand here and there to make it smooth and find bits of glass and seaweed to decorate the castle.

It wasn't very big after all. Bill said it was because Mollie and John weren't big or strong enough to dig as he could. Mollie thought he hadn't dug much, but she didn't like to say so.

"What about a bathe?" said John, who was longing to go into the calm blue water. "I'd like that."

49

"Yes, that would be fun," said Mollie. "Have you got that floating bed you talked about, Bill?"

"Yes, it's in our hut," said Bill, but he didn't seem to want to fetch it. So Mollie went to the hut and got it out. It certainly was a fine bed. It was blown up and full of air, all ready to take out on the sea. What fun! Mollie hoped she wouldn't be pushed off too often.

Soon they were all in bathing-suits. Mollie and John had theirs under their clothes, so they didn't take long to get ready. They waited for Bill, who was in the hut. He came out at last.

"Let's run straight in and dive under a big wave," said John. He and Mollie raced into the sea, and threw themselves under a big, green curling wave. Oh, how lovely! The water felt cold at first, but the children were soon warm with swimming.

Bill didn't dive in as they had done. He stood up to his knees – and he shivered! Mollie couldn't help laughing. "Come on, Bill!" she called. "It's lovely. You said you had already been in twice, and it must have been colder earlier in the day. It's warm now."

Bill went a little farther – and a bit farther. Really, if Mollie and John hadn't known he was a fine swimmer they would have thought he was just a baby At last he was in. He made a great show of splashing about, but he didn't go out very far.

"Come on out here," called John, who was quite enjoying himself in deep water. "You can't feel the bottom out here."

"I'm going to lie on the bed," said Bill. He fetched the red floating bed and lay on it. Then he called Mollie and said she could have a turn, but no sooner was she on than he tipped her off, splash!

Then John climbed on and Bill tipped him off too, splash! But nobody could tip Bill off – he was too big and heavy.

"It's cold if we don't swim about," said Molly. "Come on, John, let Bill float about if he wants to. We'll go for a swim."

So off they went. Bill lay down on the bed, shut his eyes, and let himself float up and down on the waves. The sun was warm on the bed. Bill fell asleep. He didn't hear Mollie and John yelling to him. He didn't wake up for fifteen minutes, and by that time the bed had floated almost to the big rock that Bill had pointed to so proudly when he had told Mollie and John that he had swum there and back.

Bill sat up in a fright. He stared round at the sea. Oooh!

He had floated out ever so far! He would never be able to swim back! Oh, he would be drowned! Oh, he would float to America! He would – he would! Bill burst into tears and yelled for help.

"Swim back, silly, swim back!" shouted Mollie and John. "You said you could swim as far as that rock this morning. Go on, jump in, and swim."

But Bill didn't. He sat and wept loudly on the bed.

"I say, Mollie, I don't believe the silly chap was speaking the truth when he said he was such a fine swimmer," said John suddenly. "You know what a baby he was about getting into the water – well, no good swimmer does that sort of thing. I think he was just boasting. What shall we do?"

"John, you swim after the bed, and see if you can get hold of it and guide it towards that rock," said Mollie. "I'll get the boat that Bill was in and row after you. I can get to the rock, I think and we'll all row back."

"Can you manage the boat, Mollie?" said John, swimming off. "You've never tried a boat before, you know."

"I've seen other people do it," said Mollie. "I'll be all right. Go on after Bill, quickly."

So John swam hard after the floating bed. He caught it at last and then swim to the rock, pushing the bed in front of him. Bill sat and howled on the bed. He wouldn't jump out into the water and help John. He just behaved like a silly baby.

John managed to get to the rock that stuck up out of the water. He sat on it, panting. Bill got off the bed and sat on the rock too. John dragged the bed up to them. He soon got his breath and turned to look at Bill, whose eyes were all red with crying.

"Why didn't you jump off the bed and swim to shore with it when you saw you were floating out?" asked John.

"I can't swim so far," said Bill sulkily, going red.

"Then you are a silly boaster," said John. "And a baby besides. Fancy howling like this! For goodness' sake, stop before Mollie comes. Look at her, bringing that boat out all by herself to rescue us. She's never been in a boat before, but she's rowing as well as a sailor could!"

So she was! She was pulling at the oars well, and although she was small she managed that boat beautifully. She reached the rock at last and the two boys got in.

"Now you take the oars and row back, Bill," said John.

51

JOHN SWAM HARD AFTER THE FLOATING BED

"Mollie's tired, and so am I. She's had a long row, and I've had a long swim. You've only had a good long float."

"I can't row as far as that," said Bill, redder than ever. Mollie and John stared at him in amazement.

"Well, you jolly well row as far as you can," said John. "Lazy creature! Go on, take the oars, and row! If you think I or Mollie are going to row you back all the way, you're wrong. We may rest here for a while and swim back ourselves. You can have the boat!"

"Oh, no, John, oh, no!" said Bill, beginning to cry again. "Don't do that. I'll row as best I can."

So he took the oars and began. But he couldn't row a bit! The boat hardly moved at all!

In the end John took the oars and rowed them back to shore. And there, waiting for them, was Bill's father.

"Well, young man," he said sternly to Bill, "you've made a fine baby of yourself this morning, haven't you? Had to have this youngster swimming after you to get you and the bed – and this little girl to fetch you in a boat – and then you couldn't even row back! And you've had the boat for three years now!"

Bill stood on the sand looking very small indeed, although he was such a big chap. Mollie and John stared at him in surprise and disgust, remembering the wonderful tales he had told them of the things he could do.

"Come along in and get your lunch now," said Bill's father. "As for the bed and the boat, these children shall have them for themselves whilst they are down here. It is quite clear that you are not big enough to use them!"

Bill went home. So did Mollie and John.

"I say, it's fun to have a boat and that bed to use!" said Mollie gleefully. "But I'm sorry for Bill. He was awfully silly."

"Let's be decent to him," said John. "We won't say a single word to him about to-day, but in future, Mollie, he's got to do as *we* tell him, and if he begins to boast we'll just laugh – and laugh and laugh!"

So now Bill doesn't boast any more and is very much nicer. He can swim much better, and since Mollie and John have made him take his turn at the oars, he rows quite well too. It *is* silly to boast, isn't it? – especially when you can't do what you're boasting about!

## CHAPTER THIRTEEN

# *A shock for Lucy Ann!*

Lucy Ann was a perfect nuisance. She was always putting her nose into other people's businesses, and interfering in other people's affairs.

"Oh, go away, Lucy Ann!" the children said, when she tried to show them how much better it would be to do things her way and not theirs. "You are always interfering!"

"Oh, run away, Lucy Ann!" her mother would say, when Lucy Ann came poking round, telling her mother that this corner was not dusted, and that picture was hanging all crooked. "I don't need you to come poking your nose everywhere! I can see dusty corners and crooked pictures for myself!"

"Oh, Lucy Ann, please go home!" said Mrs. Brown, who lived down the road. "I don't need *you* to tell me that my garden needs weeding, and that my roses need watering. You are always putting your nose into things that are no business of yours. Go away!"

Lucy Ann frowned and went away. But she didn't stop putting her nose into everything. She made herself such a little nuisance that no one wanted her with them.

One day, as she was coming home over the fields, she heard voices talking, and she looked about to see where they came from. To her surprise she saw four little men sitting under the hedge, making daisy chains. But they were not making them in the way that Lucy Ann made them! Instead of stringing the stalks together, they were threading the daisies through their heads.

"Oh!" said Lucy Ann, poking her nose into their play at once, "that's wrong! You shouldn't thread daisies that way! You want to do them like this!"

She snatched the daisies out of the hands of the surprised little men, and began to make holes through their stalks with a pin. The men jumped to their feet in anger – and then Lucy Ann saw that they were brownies. She stared at them, for she had never seen brownies before.

"You nasty, interfering little girl, poking your nose into our affairs!" cried one. "Your nose wants seeing to – it's much too sharp!"

"Let's make it sharper still, so that when she goes about interfering and putting her nose where it isn't wanted, she'll always know!" cried the smallest brownie. He reached out his bony little hand and smacked Lucy Ann sharply on the nose.

> 'When you poke yourself here,
> And poke yourself there,
> Just grow longer and sharper
> And make people stare,'

cried the brownie at the top of his voice.

"Oh!" cried Lucy Ann in a rage, for the slap hurt her. She was just going to slap the brownie back when there came a puff of smoke from somewhere that hid the four little men – and when the smoke cleared away, the brownies had vanished.

Lucy Ann went home, very angry. Silly little men! She had only tried to show them the right way to make a daisy chain.

Just as she was nearly home she saw two boys she knew, playing marbles on the pavement. She stopped to watch.

"Oh, you silly!" she said to one. "You will never win if you play like that. This is what you should do!"

As she was speaking a curious thing happened. Her nose grew very long indeed and very sharp. It poked itself among the marbles.

"Look! Look!" screamed the two boys, in fright. "Look at Lucy Ann's nose! It's like an elephant's trunk!"

Lucy Ann shrieked too. It was dreadful to feel her nose waving about like that! She ran home crying loudly. But by the time she was indoors her nose had gone back to its right size again, and her mother laughed at her when Lucy Ann told her what had happened.

But she didn't laugh when she saw it happen again! And it soon did. It was when Lucy Ann's mother was busy reading a letter. Lucy Ann came and peeped to see what was in the letter, for she simply couldn't keep out of anything!

"Who's it from?" she said – and, dear me, just as she said

that her nose shot out again, long and sharp and waving, and patted itself on to the letter.

Lucy Ann's mother gave a shriek. "Oh!" she cried, "how dreadful you look, Lucy Ann! Whatever has happened to your nose?"

Lucy Ann began to cry again. She told her mother about the brownies, and her mother nodded and frowned.

"Yes, you offended the little folk," she said, "and they punished you. Now your nose will always grow long and sharp whenever you poke it where it isn't wanted. Oh, Lucy Ann, what a dreadful, dreadful thing! You had better come with me to old Mother Eleanor's. She knows a bit about magic and may put it right for you."

So, crying bitterly, Lucy Ann went to Mother Eleanor's with her mother. But when Mother Eleanor heard what had happened, she laughed.

"I *could* take the spell out of her nose in a jiffy!" she said. "But I shan't!"

"Oh, but what will poor Lucy Ann do!" cried her mother.

"Do?" said Mother Eleanor. "Why, keep it right herself, of course! It only grows long and sharp when she pokes it where it isn't wanted, doesn't it? Well, if she stops poking her nose into everything it won't grow long and wave about like that "

Lucy Ann went home with her mother, and thought hard. Her nose would never be cured – unless she cured it herself! She had better try. She wouldn't interfere with any one. She would be sensible and say nothing, even when she badly wanted to poke her nose in somewhere!

Poor Lucy Ann! It wasn't so easy as she thought! Every day her nose shot out long and sharp, and every day people screamed at her or laughed loudly. But at last she tried so hard that a whole week went by and her nose stayed its right size and shape. And then she forgot again and out it shot, long and sharp, sticking itself here and there!

Lucy Ann was ashamed. She tried hard again – and, do you know, she hasn't let her nose grow long for more than a year now! She has gone to a new school, where the children don't know anything about the spell in her nose. I do hope she doesn't poke it where it isn't wanted again – because those children *will* be surprised to see what happens, won't they?

# CHAPTER FOURTEEN

## *The little piggy-boy*

There was once a little boy called Podgy because he was so fat. It was his own fault that he was too fat, for he was greedy and ate far too much.

He always had three helpings of puddings, and ate at least six cakes at tea-time. He spent all his pennies on sweets, and he was always running into the house to beg for a biscuit or an apple to eat.

"Podgy, you are a little piggy-boy," his mother said to him. "Pigs are greedy creatures, always eating, eating, eating, and growing as fat as butter. But you should not be like them, for you are not a pig but a little boy. Do not be so greedy."

But Podgy took no notice. He gobbled up his pudding and asked for more. He gobbled up his cakes and asked for more. He gobbled up his sweets and asked for more.

Now when Christmas night came Podgy hung up not one stocking, but three. He was going to be greedy over his presents, you see, as well as over his food!

"Perhaps Santa Claus will think there are three little children here, not one," thought Podgy, as he hung up his stockings. "And so I shall get three lots of presents!"

He went to sleep early, for he had had an enormous supper of bread and milk and cake. He slept and slept and slept – and what awoke him he never knew. But he found himself wide awake just as Santa Claus was standing by his stockings, ready to fill them.

Podgy sat up in bed in great excitement. Santa Claus had an enormous sack on the floor beside him, and out of the top of it all kinds of toys were peeping. Podgy leaned over to see what Santa Claus was putting into his stockings. The moonlight shone brightly down through the window and he could see everything as clearly as in daylight.

To his great surprise Santa Claus was just squeezing a large turnip into one of the stockings! Podgy watched in astonishment. Then he saw Santa Claus take two or three potatoes out of his pocket and put them into another stocking. Potatoes! Why not toys? What *could* Santa Claus be thinking of?

"I say!" said Podgy. "I say! Aren't you making a mistake, Santa Claus? Why are you putting those queer things into my stockings?"

Santa Claus turned round. "Hallo, you are awake?" he said. "Well, what else should I put into your stocking? Pigs don't like toys, surely?"

"But I'm not a pig, I'm a little boy," said Podgy, in surprise. "Can't you see that I am?"

"No, I can't," said Santa Claus, staring at him. "You look just like a little pink pig to me. Certainly you have got pyjamas on, but all the same you look exactly like a pig. Your voice sounds piggy, too – sort of grunty, you know. I was rather puzzled when I saw you lying there in bed, because people don't usually give beds to pigs – they live in stys, you know. But I thought maybe you were a pet pig."

"I'm *not* a pig, not even a pet one!" cried Podgy angrily. "I tell you I'm a little boy. There must be something wrong with your eyes, Santa Claus, if you can't see I'm a little boy."

"Well, I'll put my glasses on," said Santa Claus. "I don't want to make any mistake, you know. I've plenty of toys to give away – but if I come across any pets – dogs, cats, monkeys, goats, and so on – I usually leave them a few presents of turnips, bones, biscuits, or something. And I really thought you were a pig!"

He put on a pair of big glasses and looked carefully at Podgy, sitting up in bed. Then he shook his head again.

"*You've* made the mistake, not I," he said. "You most certainly are a little fat pig. I was sure of it before. You have a nice little snout, tiny piggy eyes and pretty, flappy ears. I expect, if you would only get out of bed and show me, you have a nice curly tail, too. You are just a nice little pet pig, and it's no use telling me any different."

Podgy slipped down into his bed and began to cry. Santa Claus took no more notice of him. He finished filling the stockings, and then disappeared up the chimney. He was gone! Podgy heard the tinkling of sleigh bells in the distance.

Podgy got out of bed and emptied his stockings. He was not going to let his mother see what Santa Claus had put in his

58

stockings. She would say, "Well, there you are, Podgy! What did I say? Didn't I tell you you were a little piggy-boy! No wonder Santa Claus couldn't tell that you were a little boy! You are as fat as a little pig because you are so greedy! If you behave like a piggy-wig, you can't expect people to think you are anything else!"

So Podgy emptied his stockings and threw all the turnips, the carrots, and the potatoes out of the window. Then he went back to bed.

In the morning how surprised his mother was to find that his stockings were quite empty.

"Santa Claus cannot have been in the night!" she said. "He must have forgotten you, Podgy, dear! Never mind – I have some nice presents for you myself."

Podgy didn't say a word. He thanked his mother for her presents when she gave them to him at breakfast-time, but not a word about Santa Claus did he say.

And after that he was careful not to be greedy. He became much less fat. He grew into a nice little boy, and he didn't look in the least like a pig – and now he is hoping that this Christmastime Santa Claus will think he looks like a little boy and fill his stockings with toys instead of turnips. Do you think he will?

## CHAPTER FIFTEEN

### The bad little doll

Kathleen was in disgrace. She had taken her little new scissors out of her work-basket and had done a lot of very naughty snipping with them! She had snipped a piece out of Mother's new curtains. She had snipped a hole in the carpet. She had even snipped a hole in a pair of Daddy's trousers!

Mother was very cross, and she had sent Kathleen to the nursery alone. Kathleen wouldn't say she was sorry, and she was so rude and sulky that Mother felt quite unhappy.

"You must go and sit alone in the nursery and think by

yourself for a little while," said Mother. "Then perhaps you will feel sorry for doing such unkind things."

Kathleen sat down on the floor and sulked. "I don't care what I did!" she said. "I snipped the carpet and the curtain and Daddy's trousers, and I don't care if I did! So there!"

There was nobody to hear her except her toys. Among her toys was a bad little doll called Twinkle. She had a bright pink face, red hair, and a green frock and green shoes. She had a cheeky smile, and the other toys thought she was very naughty.

When she heard Kathleen boasting about the naughty things she had done with the scissors Twinkle thought it would be fun to do the same! So what do you suppose that bad little doll did? She ran to the work-basket, took out the same scissors that Kathleen had been using, and looked round to see what she could snip.

"I'll snip the new cot-cover that Kathleen knitted the other day!" thought naughty Twinkle. So she ran to the doll's cot, and snipped a big hole in the pretty green cover. Kathleen suddenly saw her running and snipping, and she stared in surprise and dismay.

"Twinkle! Oh, Twinkle! How very horrid of you! You've cut the beautiful new cot-cover, I made – and it took me *so* long to knit it! Oh, you horrid doll!"

Twinkle laughed, and ran away from Kathleen. She went to the doll's house and peeped inside. Good! She would snip the new curtains there! Kathleen had hung them up only the day before. She had made them of lace that her mother had given her. It would be fun to snip little holes in them!

Snip-snip-snip went the scissors! The curtains hung in rags now – and Kathleen suddenly caught sight of them.

"Twinkle! You've snipped holes in my nice new curtains! Oh, you unkind, horrid little doll! Come here! Give me those scissors! Oh, you deserve a good smacking, you bad little doll!"

Twinkle ran out of the doll's house and looked round for some more mischief to do. What about snipping the golliwog's red coat? He had his back to her, and she could snip a piece from the bottom of it!

Twinkle ran to the golliwog and snip-snip-snip went her scissors! The golliwog turned round in dismay.

"Oh! Twinkle! You've cut my best coat! Just look what she's done, Kathleen – she's spoilt my coat!"

60

TWINKLE RAN TO THE GOLLIWOG AND SNIP, SNIP
WENT HER SCISSORS

61

Kathleen put out her hand and caught the naughty doll – and Twinkle snipped a hole in Kathleen's pretty blue frock! Wasn't it dreadful of her?

"I shall smack you and put you in the corner!" said Kathleen, half crying. "You've spoilt my cot-cover, you've cut holes in my new curtains, you've snipped Golly's coat, and now you've made a hole in my dress! Aren't you sorry for all you've done, you naughty doll?"

"No," said Twinkle sulkily. "It was nice snipping things with the scissors. I'm not a bit sorry."

Just then Mother came in, and how surprised she was to find Kathleen crying and her doll Twinkle on her lap looking very sulky indeed.

"Twinkle is a bad little doll, Mother," said Kathleen. "She took my scissors and snipped holes in the cot-cover and holes in the curtains, and a piece out of Golly's coat, and made a hole in my frock too. And she won't say she's sorry. She seems quite pleased about it."

"Well, darling, you can't very well be cross with her," said Mother. "She is only doing what you did, you know. You were naughty with the scissors too – and you were rude and sulky afterwards, as well, when you saw how upset I was. You can't blame Twinkle. She is just copying you."

Kathleen stared at her mother. It was quite true! Twinkle had done exactly what she, Kathleen, had done. Now Kathleen knew what it felt like to have nice things spoilt – and to have a rude and sulky child!

"I'm sorry, Mother!" she cried, and she ran to her mother and hugged her, "I was horrid. I won't do it again. I do love you. I don't want to make you unhappy!"

Her mother kissed her and went downstairs again, feeling quite happy. Twinkle the doll looked up at Kathleen, and spoke in a little, unhappy voice.

"I'm sorry too," she said. "I was horrid. I won't do it again. I do love you. I don't want to make you unhappy!"

"Well, it was all my fault really," said Kathleen. "I can't expect my toys to behave nicely if *I* don't. Cheer up, Twinkle, and be good!"

So Twinkle was good after that – but all the same Kathleen took her scissors out of the work-basket! She knew how horrid it was to have things spoilt, and she wasn't going to let that bad little doll have her scissors any more!

## CHAPTER SIXTEEN

# Simple Simon makes a mistake

"Listen to me, Simon," said his mother one day. "I am going to take Baby to see Auntie Harriet. I shall leave you at home because your best suit is dirty and your old suit is torn. So you must be a good boy and not get in to mischief."

"No, Mother," said Simon. "I won't get into mischief. I feel quite good to-day."

"And just see that Rover the dog and Sally the cat behave themselves too," said Mother. "I don't want to find Rover's muddy paw-marks all over my clean kitchen floor. And please don't let Sally the cat get into the larder."

"Oh, no, Mother," said Simon.

"Well, good-bye, Simon," said Mother, pushing the pram down the path with Baby inside. "Just remember what I've said. You know what happens to naughty boys, don't you? They get sent to bed."

"Oh, yes, Mother," said Simon, and he waved to his mother till she was out of sight.

It was quite true that Simon did feel good that day. He wanted to be helpful and kind and nice. He pulled a mat straight in the kitchen. He went to the larder and looked to see if the lid of the bread-bin was on. He opened the oven door to see if the dinner Mother had left cooking was quite all right. Yes, really, Simon was feeling very good.

Rover barked in the yard – woof, woof, woof! Simon went to the kitchen door and looked out at him.

"You'd better be good, Rover," he called. "You know what happens when we are naughty, don't you? We get sent to bed!"

"Woof, woof!" said Rover, and he ran out into the muddy lane. Something rubbed against Simon's legs. He looked down. It was Sally the cat. Simon bent down and stroked her.

"You'd better be good too, Sally-cat," said Simon. "You

63

know what happens when we are naughty, don't you? We get sent to bed!"

"Miaow!" said Sally-cat, and she ran back to the kitchen fire. Simon went down the garden to see if there were any snowdrops peeping. But he couldn't find any. It was cold, so he went back to the kitchen.

And what do you think? Rover was in the kitchen, and had left two trails of muddy paw-marks all across Mother's clean floor. Oh dear! Simon stared at Rover in anger.

"Rover! Didn't I tell you to be good? Didn't I tell you what happens when we are naughty? You must go straight to bed! Come here!"

Rover wouldn't come. So Simon ran to him and took him by the collar. He dragged the surprised dog up the stairs and into his own bedroom. He turned back the sheet and the blankets and lifted up the heavy dog. Plonk! Simon dropped him in the bed and tucked him in tightly.

"Now you just stay there for the rest of the day!" said Simon. "You will not muddy the kitchen again, I am sure!"

He marched downstairs, feeling very important to think he had sent naughty dog Rover to bed. And when he got into the kitchen, what did he see but Sally the cat in the larder eating up the meat-pie that Mother made for Father's supper! My goodness me!

"Sally-cat! How dare you!" shouted Simon, quite forgetting that it was he who had left the larder door open. "Didn't I tell you to be good? Didn't I tell you what happens when we are naughty? You must go straight to bed! Come here!"

Sally-cat tried to jump out of the window, but Simon caught her. He did not smack her, and Sally thought he was cuddling her, so she began to purr.

"No, I am not pleased with you, Sally-cat," said Simon. "I am going to send you to bed!"

Up the stairs he climbed, and went into his bedroom. Rover was still in bed, but you should have seen the muddy marks he had made on the clean sheet. And will you believe it, he had bitten a hole in the blanket! But Simon was so cross with Sally-cat that he didn't notice what Rover had done. He pushed the cat down under the clothes and pulled the blanket up tightly. Then he left the dog and the cat together in bed and shut the door. Bang! Down the stairs he went and cleaned up the bits of meat-pie and washed up the muddy marks on the kitchen floor. He was really feeling a very good boy indeed that day!

But upstairs, oh! dear! Sally-cat didn't like being pushed down under the bedclothes with Rover the dog. They were quite good friends usually, but it was strange to be in Simon's bed. Sally-cat scratched Rover's hind leg.

"Woof!" said Rover, in alarm. He dived down under the clothes and tried to bite Sally-cat. Sally-cat scratched his nose! Then what a muddle there was in Simon's bed! The dog and the cat got all tangled up in the bed-clothes and couldn't get out! They scrambled round this way and they got tied up that way, and they scratched and bit at the blankets and sheets in fright.

But the door was shut, and Simon heard nothing. He got a book and sat down to read quietly. He was quite surprised when the door opened and his mother came home again with Baby.

"Oh, Mother, I've been such a good boy," said Simon. "I haven't got into any mischief at all."

"That's fine," said his Mother, putting Baby into her high chair.

"But, Mother, Rover was very naughty," said Simon. "He walked all across the kitchen floor with his muddy feet."

"And who left the kitchen door open so that he could do *that*?" said Mother at once.

Simon pretended not to hear. "And, Mother, Sally-cat was naughty too," he said. "She got into the larder and ate the meat-pie there!"

"And who left the larder door open so that she could do *that*?" said Mother, very cross indeed.

"Well, Mother, you'll be glad to know that I punished them both," said Simon. "I sent them to bed!"

"To *bed*!" said Mother. "Whatever do you mean, Simon?"

"I put them both to bed for the rest of the day," said Simon proudly. "They are upstairs in my bed, Mother, and I'm sure they are feeling very sorry they've been so naughty."

"Oh dear, oh dear, oh dear," said Mother, and she rushed upstairs and into Simon's bedroom What a sight she saw! There seemed to be a sort of earthquake going on in Simon's bed, and woofs and mews came from it in a most remarkable manner! Rover and Sally-cat were in a dreadful muddle there and were trying their very hardest to get out.

"The sheets are all over mud and are torn to bits!" cried Mother. "And the blankets are nibbled and torn! Oh dear, oh dear, oh dear! Shoo, Rover! Shoo, Sally-cat!"

Mother pulled the sheets and blankets off, and the dog and the cat fled downstairs in a hurry. Mother called Simon. He ran upstairs and looked at his torn and dirty bed in surprise.

"Simon, I'm going to send *you* to bed!" said Mother in her crossest voice. "Hurry up and get in! It's all dirty and torn, but that's your own fault. Putting the cat and the dog to bed indeed! Whatever will you think of next! Into bed you get, and there you'll stay all day long!"

"But, Mother, I was feeling such a good boy!" wailed poor Simon.

"You've got to *be* good as well as *feel* good!" said Mother.

And so poor Simon stayed in bed, and not even Rover or Sally-cat came to see him! But I'm not surprised at that, are you?

## CHAPTER SEVENTEEN

# *The girl who wanted everything*

There was once a little girl called Lulu. She had plenty of toys, and plenty of good things to eat, and yet she always wanted something else. If she had a curly-haired doll in her pram and saw some one else with a straight-haired doll, she wanted that. If she had a white teddy-bear and saw a brown one, she wanted that. She just wanted everything.

One day her auntie asked her what she would like for her birthday, and Lulu thought hard.

"I want a new dolly's pram," she said. "A green one, with a hood and a cover and everything."

So her auntie bought her a doll's pram, and really, it was the loveliest one you can imagine. Just like a real pram. It even had a brake on one wheel, and a green cover with "L" on it for Lulu.

Lulu was pleased. "I shall take it out this morning," she said, "and every one will see it and wish they had a pram like it."

So she took it out, and it shone very brightly in the spring sunshine. Soon she met Molly in her little red motor-car, and she called to her:

"Look at my lovely new pram! Don't you wish it was yours?"

"Well, you look at my red motor-car," said Molly. "It's better than a pram. You can get in it and ride about. But you have to push a pram. My motor-car is nicer than your pram."

Lulu felt upset. The little red motor-car did look nice. What a pity she hadn't asked her aunt for one!

"Molly, would you like my pram in exchange for your motor-car?" she said suddenly. "You haven't got a pram, have you?"

Molly hopped out of her car in a trice and took the pram-handles, her eyes shining. "You can have my car," she said. "Good-bye, Lulu." And off she went very happily.

Lulu got into the car. It was very nice, and it had a hooter she could press to make a nice "Honk-honk" sound. She rode down the street in the motor-car, honking all the way. Soon she met David and he stared at the car.

David was wheeling a fine barrow, with a bright blue wheel, a yellow body, and blue handles. It looked very grand.

"Hallo, David!" said Lulu. "Look at my lovely new motor-car! Don't you wish it was yours?"

"Well, you look at my lovely barrow," said David. "Nobody's got one like it. Do you see its blue wheel? It is so useful too – you can carry anything you like in it. It is nicer than your car."

Lulu stared crossly. The barrow did look nice. What a pity she hadn't asked her aunt for one!

"David, would you like my car in exchange for your barrow?" she said.

David ran to the car at once and helped Lulu out. Then in he got and pedalled away quickly, his face red with joy. Lulu went to wheel the barrow. It certainly was very nice. She wheeled it away.

Soon she met Amy with a new doll. It could open and shut its eyes and say "Ma-Ma!"

"Hallo, Amy," said Lulu. "Look at my new barrow. Don't you wish it was yours?"

"Well, you look at my fine doll," said Amy. "It's the only one I know that can say 'Ma-ma!' Listen!"

Lulu listened to the doll speaking and she felt cross. What a pity she hadn't asked her aunt for one like that!

"Amy, would you like my barrow in exchange for your doll?" she said.

Amy's eyes shone. She pushed the doll into Lulu's arms and took up the beautiful barrow. She ran off with it gaily. Lulu nursed the doll and went on her way, feeling pleased.

She met Jimmy, carrying a fine golliwog, and she called to him, "Hallo, Jimmy! Look at my beautiful doll! It says 'Ma-ma!' Listen!"

"Well, you look at my fine golliwog!" said Jimmy. Better than any in the town. See his nice black face? He is nicer than your doll!"

Lulu was vexed. What a pity she hadn't asked her aunt for a golliwog! "Jimmy!" she said. "Would you like my doll in exchange for your golly?"

Jimmy stared at the beautiful doll and thought how his little sister would love it. He gave his golly to Lulu and ran off with the lovely doll. Lulu was pleased to have such a nice golliwog. She went down the road singing to him, and soon she met Harry, who was sucking such a big peppermint bull's-eye that his cheek was all swollen. Lulu loved peppermints. She ran to Harry.

"Give me a peppermint," she said to Harry. "You have a whole bagful."

"No, I shan't give you one," said Harry. "You didn't give me a toffee when you had some."

Lulu felt terribly hungry for sweets. She showed Harry her golly. "See what a nice golly I have," she said. "I'll let you hold him if you'll give me a sweet."

"My sweets are nicer than any stupid golly," said Harry.

"Well, will you give me that whole bagful in exchange for the golly?" said Lulu. Harry was delighted. He quickly gave Lulu the sweets and ran off with the lovely golly. Lulu sat down on a doorstep and began to eat the sweets. She ate them all – wasn't she greedy! But that was just like Lulu. Then she went home – and found her aunt there.

"Well, where is your doll's pram?" asked her aunt.

"DAVID," SHE SAID, "WOULD YOU LIKE MY CAR IN
EXCHANGE FOR YOUR BARROW?"

Lulu went red. "I changed it for a motor-car," she said. "And then I changed that for a barrow – and I changed the barrow for a doll – and the doll for a golly – and the golly for a bag of sweets. And I've eaten the sweets."

"You bad, naughty girl!" cried her aunt. "You have given away that beautiful doll's pram – and have nothing at all to show for it. You thought the other children had nicer things than you had, so you had to have them – and now you have nothing at all! It serves you right! I will never give you a present again."

And she never did. But I don't feel very sorry for Lulu – do you?

## CHAPTER EIGHTEEN

### *The boy who grew a tail*

There was once a boy called Harry who was a dreadful tease. His mother had two cats and a dog, and every time Harry saw them anywhere near, he pulled their tails. The dog growled, and the cats spat and hissed – but Harry only laughed.

"You shouldn't do that, Harry," his mother said. "It is very unkind. One day the cats will scratch you and the dog will bite you – then you will be sorry."

"Oh, no, Mother, they won't," said Harry – and he was right. The dog was too kind-hearted to bite, and the cats did not like the idea of scratching any one belonging to the Mistress who loved and fed them. So Harry went on pulling their tails whenever he had a chance.

It wasn't a bit of good the dog sitting on his tail, for Harry just pushed him off it and then gave it a tug. The cats tried to curl their tails tightly round their bodies – but Harry uncurled them and pulled hard.

"Grrrrrrr!" said the dog.

"Mee-o-ee-ow!" squealed the cats. "Let-go-ee-ow! You hurt me so-ee-ow!"

Now one day the two cats and the dog went to see a friend

of theirs, a small pixie dog who lived with his master in a little yellow house in the heart of the wood. And they happened to tell Wagtail the dog about Harry.

"Well, well, well!" said Wagtail, who was a curious-looking dog because he had wings and could fly. "Fancy a boy pulling tails like that. Why don't you cure him?"

"We don't know how to," said the cats.

"Now listen," said Wagtail. "*I* know how to. My master has a tail-growing spell. I know all about it because once my tail got caught in a trap and came off and I had to grow a new one. There's a bit of the spell left. It's in this drawer."

Wagtail opened a drawer and took out a little box. There was some powder in it.

"Now if you could manage to put this powder into a glass of milk that Harry drinks, *he* will grow a tail," said Wagtail. "And I guess the boys and girls at his school will pull it. Then he'll know what it feels like."

The dog and the two cats took the tail-spell back home again, feeling most excited. It was quite easy to put it into a glass of milk that Harry was going to drink. Then they watched him drink it.

"What a funny taste my milk has to-day," said Harry – but he didn't know why it was.

Now, will you believe it, in the night he grew a tail  He really did. He woke up in the morning to find that he had a nice long grown tail of his own. He went and looked at himself in a mirror – and he was so surprised and upset.

"Mother! Mother! I've grown a tail in the night!" cried Harry.

"Don't be silly, dear," said his mother, thinking Harry was just having a joke. But you should have seen her stare when she saw Harry's tail  She couldn't believe her eyes.

"I don't want to go to school with a tail," said Harry, almost crying. "The others will laugh at me."

"Well, you'll have to be laughed at then," said his mother. "You shouldn't have pulled the tails of the cats and the dog so often, Harry. I knew something would happen to you one day."

So Harry had to go to school with his long brown tail. He did look funny! He tried to curl it round him as the cats did – but it was no use – the children at school soon saw it and pulled it undone.

"Harry's got a long tail! Harry's got a long tail!" they sang in delight. "Oh, what a beauty! Let's pull it."

So they pulled it hard.

"Ooooh! Ow! Don't!" squealed Harry. "It hurts."

"But it isn't a real tail, is it?" asked the children. "It's only a pretend one you've put on for fun."

"It *is* a real tail," said poor Harry, sitting down on it. But the children made him get up, and then pulled it hard again to see if they could pull it off, for they couldn't believe it was a real tail.

Of course Harry's tail wouldn't come off, because it was growing – and it hurt him dreadfully to have it pulled. He began to cry. But the school bell rang just then and all the children went in to their places. Harry sat down hard on his tail. He didn't mean to have it pulled again.

But do you know, when playtime came the children made up a game of "Pull-his-tail!" and they made Harry run round the playground, and they chased him to see who could pull his tail before he got round. Harry was dreadfully upset – but he couldn't stop the children. It hurt him very much every time his tail was pulled, and he yelled loudly. "Ooooh-ee-ow!"

"He's mewing like a cat!" cried the boys and girls. "Listen to him! Pull his tail again."

"Ooooh-ee-ow!" squealed poor Harry. The children laughed and shouted. They thought it was a fine new game. They were quite sure that Harry was only pretending to have a tail – they didn't think he was really being hurt.

When Harry went home, crying and unhappy, he sat down in a corner of the sitting-room and thought hard. So that was what it was like to have a tail pulled! No wonder the dog and the cats had squealed and run away from him so often. Big tears ran down Harry's cheeks. Was he to have this horrid brown tail all his life – and go about having it pulled? It was dreadful.

The dog saw the little boy crying in the corner. He went over to him and licked his hand. He didn't like to see Harry crying. The cats saw that he was sad too, and they went over to sit on his knee.

"I'm crying because I've got a tail like you," said Harry, wiping his eyes. "And I don't like it, because every one pulls it and it hurts me very much. I'm sorry I pulled your tails now. I'll never, never do it again, now that I know how it hurts."

The dog licked his hand again and looked at the two cats. "Woof, woof, woof," said the dog to the cats in a low voice. "Mee-ow-ee-ow-ee-ow!" said the cats. And that meant, "Shall we try to get the spell away?" "Yes, we certainly will."

So off they went to their friend Wagtail again and told him what a bad time Harry had had, and how he had said he was sorry he had pulled their tails and would never do it again.

"Well," said Wagtail, "you let him keep that tail of his. It will do him good to wear it till it falls off, which will be in two weeks' time. It will serve him right."

"No," said the dog. "Tell us how to take it away, please, Wagtail. Harry is very unhappy. We have forgiven him for the times he has pulled our tails. It is no use being unkind to him because he was so many times unkind to us, now that he is sorry."

"Oh, very well," said Wagtail. "All you have to do is to get Harry to sit with his back to a pail of hot water. Put his tail into it – and it will melt away. It's quite easy."

So back went the dog and the two cats and got a pail of hot water. Harry was astonished to see them so busy with it. But he was even more astonished when the dog came up to him with the water and put it behind the stool he was sitting on. The cats lifted up his long brown tail and put it into the water. Harry stared in surprise. What could they all be doing? But he guessed it was something magic, so he sat quite still, his heart beating fast.

And do you know, his tail melted all away just as if it were a piece of brown sugar. It got smaller and smaller and thinner and thinner. It melted away to nothing. It turned the water a bright green, which was strange because the tail was brown. It was gone

Harry stood up and looked round. Yes – his tail was certainly gone. How glad he was! He hugged the dog and the two cats for joy, and then went to empty the green water away. He wasn't going to have any tail-magic left about the house.

He told his mother what had happened. "What a very surprising thing!" she said. "Well, it's a good thing your tail's gone, Harry. I don't expect you'll pull the animals' tails any more now."

"No, I shan't," said Harry. "I know what it feels like! I'm sorry I ever did it."

"Well, be careful you don't do it again without thinking," said his mother. "Or *your* tail might grow once more."

It hasn't grown again – so I expect Harry has remembered all right, don't you? I do hope he won't forget. He might grow a peacock's tail next time, and that *would* be awkward!

## CHAPTER NINETEEN

# *Disobedient Peter*

Peter was proud of his new paddling-shoes. They were green, and on each toe there was a white piece of rubber in the shape of a little ship.

"Aren't they nice?" said Peter's mother. "Now listen, dear. I want you to wear these little rubber shoes *on* the beach as well as when you paddle."

"Oh, why, Mummy?" said Peter. "I do like to feel the sand with my feet."

"I know you do," said Mummy. "But yesterday I saw some broken glass on the beach, and I heard of a little girl who cut her foot on a piece. So I want you to keep your paddling-shoes on."

"People shouldn't leave broken glass about," said Peter. "It makes us wear shoes when we don't want to."

"It is very careless of people," said Mummy. "But as I don't want you to get your feet cut, Peter, I'd like you to keep your shoes on, and to paddle in them too. Now don't forget."

Peter loved paddling. It *was* fun to go splish-splashing through the tiny waves. The stones didn't hurt his feet when he had his paddling-shoes on. Sometimes there was sand and sometimes there were stones. He didn't mind which if he had his shoes on.

Now that afternoon Mummy left Peter on the beach with Tinker the dog. "I'm going to get some cakes for tea," she said. "Play here nicely with Tinker, Peter, and I will come down to you as soon as I can."

Peter thought he would build a castle. He soon began, and Tinker got very excited and tried to dig too, sending the sand up into the air like a shower of spray.

"Hie! Stop, stop, Tinker!" said Peter. "That's not helping me! I don't like sand in my eyes."

The sand was warm in the sun. Peter's feet felt hot. He looked down at his new shoes.

"I wish I could take you off," he said. "You do make my feet hot."

"Woof!" said Tinker, and put his paw on Peter's foot.

"Yes, you needn't show me that you don't wear shoes," said Peter. "I know it already. On dear! I really think I'll take my shoes off for a little while. If I stay just here and don't go running over the beach I shall be all right."

So he took them off and set them neatly by his castle. Then he went on building it up, higher and higher and higher.

And do you know, by the time the castle was finished, the sea was almost up to it. Peter was so excited! He shouted for joy. "I shall stand on top – I shall be king of the castle! Hurrah!"

He stood right on the top of his castle. He had made it very firmly indeed, and patted it down well, so it was a very strong castle.

And then Peter suddenly remembered his paddling-shoes. "Oh dear! I must put them on again," he said. So he scrambled down to find them. But he must have put sand on top of them, because they couldn't be seen anywhere.

Mummy came down to the beach, and shouted in surprise to see Peter's enormous castle. "What a big one!" she cried.

"Oh, Mummy, I've lost my shoes," said Peter in dismay, as he looked for them.

"But I told you not to take them off," said Mummy, quite cross.

"Well, my feet were very hot, and I thought if I stayed here, just in one place, it wouldn't matter if I took them off for a little while," said Peter, going red.

"That was very naughty of you," said Mummy. "I trusted you not to. Hurry up and find them and put them on."

But just then an enormous wave came and ran right round the castle – splosh! Peter only just jumped up in time or he would have been soaked through. Mummy had to run ever so far back.

As soon as the wave had gone back, Peter got down from the castle and hunted about for his shoes once more – but there wasn't any sign of them at all.

"The sea must have taken them," said the little boy sadly. "They're not here. Tinker, can't you find them?"

But Tinker couldn't, though he hunted too. Soon the sea was so far up the beach that Peter had to leave his castle and go and sit by the wall with Mummy. She had his walking shoes with her and he put them on.

"I suppose I can't paddle in these shoes," said Peter in a sad voice.

"Of course not," said Mummy. "That's the worst of not doing as you are told – something horrid always happens! I am not going to punish you, because your shoes have punished you by getting lost, so that you can't paddle again."

Peter was very upset. It was such fun to paddle. He sat by Mummy, looking very red. The sea made nice little waves and ran almost up to Peter. But he couldn't go and splash in them because he had lost his paddling-shoes.

Soon it was time to go home to tea. There was a little girl at the same house as Peter was staying at, and when she came in to tea her face was red with crying. Peter wondered why. But he didn't like to ask her. He thought perhaps she had lost her paddling shoes too – but she hadn't, because he saw them by her spade.

"What are we going to do after tea, Mummy?" asked Peter.

"We'll go for a walk over the cliff and fly your kite," Mummy said. "It's always so windy there."

"Oooh!" said Peter, pleased. It was fun to fly his kite up on the cliff. The wind pulled hard and the kite flew very high.

After tea he went to speak to Mollie, the little girl. "Where's your new pail?" he said.

Tears came into Mollie's eyes. "Oh, Peter," she said, "when I was playing with it this afternoon a big wave came and took it away. I couldn't get it back, and now it's lost. And it was such a lovely one."

"Oh, what a pity!" said Peter. "It was the one with Mickey Mouse on, wasn't it?"

"Yes," said Mollie. "I'm going to look for it on the beach after tea. Mummy says it may be left there when the tide goes down. Will you come and help me to look, Peter?"

PETER ONLY JUST JUMPED UP IN TIME

"I'm going to fly my kite with Mummy, on the cliff," said Peter.

"Oh, I do wish you weren't," said Mollie. "If only you'd help me I'm I sure could find my pail. But the beach is so big to look all by myself."

Peter was a kind little boy. He badly wanted to fly his kite – but Mollie did need his help very badly too.

"Well – I'll come and help you instead of flying my kite," he said. "I lost my paddling-shoes this afternoon, so I know how horrid it is to lose something. I'll go and tell Mummy, and then we'll go to the beach together."

So in a little while Mollie and Peter were hunting all over the beach to see if the pail had been left by the tide. The sea had gone down, and was leaving big stretches of sea-weed, shells, and rubbish in crooked lines here and there. Peter and Mollie wandered up and down the long beach, looking hard.

It was dull work. Peter wished he was up on the cliff with Mummy, flying his kite. He was sure he would not see Mollie's pail. It would be just a waste of time.

But suddenly he *did* see it! It was under a pile of brown seaweed. He could quite well see a bit of Micky Mouse's red coat showing there. He ran to it with a shout.

"I've got your pail – I've got your pail!" he cried. He pulled it out of the seaweed – and oh, whatever do you suppose was inside the pail? Guess! Yes – one of Peter's green paddling shoes!

"Oh! oh!" squealed Peter in delight. "Here's one of my shoes in your pail, Mollie. Oh! Let's look for the other one. It's sure to be near."

The two excited children looked hard – and soon Mollie gave a shout. "I've got it – I've got it! Look, it's under this little rock! It's full of shells! Oh, Peter, aren't we lucky! We've found all the things we lost."

They rushed home to their mothers. How pleased they were!

"Well, Peter, if you hadn't given up your kite-flying to help Mollie, I don't suppose either the pail or your shoes would have been found," said Mummy, hugging him. "So, though you were disobedient and lost your shoes, your kindness got them back. One was waiting for you in Mollie's pail – that *was* funny!"

# CHAPTER TWENTY

## *The silly girl*

Ellen, Jack, and Barbara were staying at the seaside. Oh, what fun it was! You should have seen the castles they built, the big pools they made, and the fun they had paddling out in the little waves!

It was warm weather, so they all wore sun-suits, with a jersey on the top if the sun went in. It was fun wearing a sun-suit, because if they wanted to bathe all they had to do was to run straight into the water, splash about for a while, and then come out and put on dry sun-suits.

But do you know, Barbara was such a silly-billy. She didn't like bathing.

"Barbara, do come in!" Jack would call. "It's simply lovely. You're missing such a lot of fun."

"It's too cold," Barbara would say, standing on the edge of the water. "I don't like it."

"But you don't notice it when you're in!" the others would shout. "Oh, do come in! It's so lovely!"

But Barbara just stood paddling on the edge and wouldn't go in with the others. So after a bit they left her alone at bathing-time, and just had fun by themselves.

Then two other children came along with a funny horse made of rubber. You could ride in the water on this horse, and it was such fun trying to tip the rider off. Jack and Ellen shouted with laughter every time any one fell off it.

Barbara still stood at the edge, and she watched them playing. "Come along, Barbara!" cried Jack. "You can have a turn too at riding on the rubber horse. It feels so jolly, bumping up and down on the waves."

"Bring it here to me," said Barbara. But the children who had brought the horse shook their heads.

"It won't float properly in such shallow water," said George.

"It just turns over on its side in those little tiny waves," said Susie. "Come along, Barbara! Do have a turn."

But Barbara just wouldn't go out and bathe properly. "You're a silly girl!" said Jack.

"Yes, you're really silly, Barbara," said Ellen. "You are missing all the fun."

Now the next day Barbara saw a fine big rubber ball in a shop. It was blue, red, and yellow, and was a marvellous bouncer. Barbara had a shilling of her own and she bought the ball. She bounced it all the way to the beach – it was lovely!

"Oh, we'll have some fine games on the sand with this ball!" cried Barbara. "Come on, Jack! Come on, Ellen! We'll play football."

Very soon Jack, Ellen, Barbara, George, and Susie were playing football with the new ball. It raced along the sands as if it were alive. It was a fine ball. When it bounced it shot high above Barbara's head. She was very proud of the ball.

Soon Jack said it was time to bathe. "Come on!" he shouted to the others. "Bathing-time! The sea is lovely this morning."

In he went, splish-splash, shouting with joy. Ellen rushed after him, and George and Susie went so fast that George tripped and fell headlong in the waves. How the others laughed! George was up in a trice, and began to splash.

Barbara stood at the edge as usual, watching the others. She really was a little silly, wasn't she! She did so long to join the play – it looked such fun!

She began to throw her ball up into the air and catch it. She missed it – and it rolled into the sea. The wind was blowing strongly, and it blew the ball out of Barbara's reach.

Barbara ran after the ball, splashing up to her knees in the little waves. She stopped to get the ball – but the wind blew it a little farther away.

"My ball! my ball!" cried Barbara. The others were so busy playing that they didn't hear her. Barbara splashed farther out after her ball. She was right over her knees now – but still the ball went farther away, bobbing up and down on the waves just as if it were having a fine game with Barbara.

"Oh, do come back!" shouted Barbara to the ball. But it didn't. It bobbed even farther out. Barbara waded out after it. The water was almost up to her waist. But Barbara didn't notice that. She reached out her hand to grab the ball – and a little wave bobbed it away from her.

Now Barbara was above her waist in water. She didn't care. She only thought of getting that ball somehow. She couldn't, couldn't lose her beautiful new ball that had cost a whole shilling! The ball bobbed out to sea, and Barbara went on wading after it.

Do you know, the water was right up to her shoulders before she got up to her ball. Yes – only her head showed above the water. She was out even deeper than the others – too deep, really, because she could only swim just a little bit.

Suddenly the others missed seeing Barbara at the edge of the water. "Where's Barbara?" cried Ellen.

"She's gone!" said Jack. "Oh dear – isn't she a silly? Here we've been having a perfectly lovely time bathing and silly old Barbara must have gone home because she was lonely. I do wish she'd bathe properly."

"Look! Barbara *is* bathing!" cried George in surprise, and he pointed over the water to where Barbara was, just up to her shoulders. "Oooh! Isn't she in deep water! Barbara, come back! You're too deep!"

But Barbara was enjoying herself. Now that she was right in the water, she found it was lovely and warm just as the others had said. She didn't want to go out.

She waved to the others. "I'm going to try and swim!" she said. "Catch the ball and keep it safe for me!"

She threw the ball to Jack and he caught it. Then she flung herself forward in the water and began to strike out with her arms and legs.

"Barbara's swimming – look, Barbara's swimming!" cried the others. "Oh, Barbara, you are clever!"

Didn't Barbara enjoy herself! How nice it was to have all the others admiring her, thinking she was brave and clever, instead of calling her a silly!

They all ran out to the rocks to change their sun-suits and dry themselves. Barbara took her ball from Jack and set it down carefully.

"Barbara, why did you think you would bathe this morning after all?" asked Jack. "Did you suddenly feel very brave or something?"

Barbara wished she *could* say she had felt brave – but she was a truthful little girl, so she shook her head.

"No," she said, "it was my new ball that made me bathe. It floated away on the sea, and I had to go after it. And by the time I had got it I was up to my shoulders in water, and I hadn't noticed it was cold or anything. So as I was in, I thought I might as well stay in and enjoy myself."

"Oh! We shall know what to do to-morrow when we bathe!" cried George. "We'll throw Barbara's ball into the water and she'll have to go after it."

"No, don't do that," said Barbara. "I shan't be silly any more. If a ball can make me go in and enjoy it, I can make myself. I'll come in every day now and play with you all. My ball has shown me how to."

And now Barbara bathes properly every day with the others, and loves it. Wasn't she a silly-billy at first?

## CHAPTER TWENTY-ONE

### *The magic hummybugs*

There were once two naughty little children, called Thomas and Polly. They were both greedy, and if they could possibly take a cake from the cake-tin, a biscuit from the biscuit-jar, or a sweet when nobody was looking, they did.

So you see they were not at all honest. Sometimes they were caught and well spanked, and sometimes they were not caught. Their mother was unhappy about them, but she couldn't seem to make them any better.

But one day they took sweets belonging to old Dame Quick-Eyes – ah, that was a silly thing to do! I'll tell you all about it.

Dame Quick-Eyes lived in a little cottage all by herself. She sometimes did people's washing, and she sometimes did people's mending. Polly often took her a basket of socks and stockings to darn, and the old dame was glad of the work to do. She had such good eyes that she could see perfectly well without spectacles.

Now one morning, on their way to school, Thomas and Polly had to leave some pillow-cases for Dame Quick-Eyes to wash. They knocked at her door but nobody answered.

"She's out!" said Polly. "Shall we leave the parcel on her doorstep?"

"No – we'll put it in at the kitchen window," said Thomas. "It's usually open."

So they went round to the back and, sure enough, the kitchen window was open. Polly pushed the parcel on to the table there – and then she caught sight of something.

It was a bag of humbugs! Do you know what humbugs are like? They are those lovely big, striped peppermint sweets that last such a long time! Well, Dame Quick-Eyes was very fond of humbugs, and always had a bag of them by her side when she did her mending. And there was the bag she had bought the day before, lying on the table.

"Ooooh!" said Polly and Thomas at the same moment, staring at the lovely bag of humbugs.

"Let's take one each," said Thomas. "She won't know."

So those bad children took one big humbug each, out of Dame Quick-Eyes' bag. They were big black-and-white striped sweets, and the children knew they would not have time to suck them before they got to school. So Thomas tore two pages out of a notebook he carried, and wrapped one humbug up for himself, and one for Polly. Polly put hers in her pocket and Thomas put away his. They meant to suck them at playtime.

Off they went to school. They took off their hats and coats and went to take their places. Thomas sat in the middle of the class, and Polly sat at the back.

Now, although the children didn't know it, those humbugs had been bought at a little pixie sweet-shop in the middle of Ho-Ho Wood. Dame Quick-Eyes sometimes did washing for the pixies there, and she always bought her sweets at his shop because they were so delicious.

Now those pixie humbugs had a little magic in them that made them hum whenever they got warm. You may have wondered why they should be called *hum*bugs – well, of course, it is because any bit of magic in them makes them *hum* loudly as soon as they get warm. In Fairyland they are called hummy-bugs, but we just call them humbugs for short.

Well, it wasn't long before the humbugs in the two children's pockets began to get warm. So, of course, they started to hum!

"Zzzzzzzzzz!" went the humbug in Thomas's pocket and "Zzzzzzzzzz!" went the one in Polly's. The two children opened their eyes wide in surprise when they heard this noise. It sounded like a bumble-bee buzzing. Polly and Thomas looked around their desk to see if a bee was there.

"Zzzzzzz-zzzz!" said Thomas's humbug loudly.

"Zzzzzzzzzzz!" said Polly's humbug too.

"Who is making that noise?" said the teacher angrily.

Nobody said a word, except the two humbugs. And they answered cheerfully and loudly: "Zzzzzzzzzz! Zzzzzzzz!"

"Somebody is humming!" said the teacher.

Somebody – or something – certainly was!

"Zzzzzzzzzzzz!" Every one stared at Thomas and Polly, for there was no doubt the noise came from them.

"Thomas! Polly! Stop making that noise at once!" said the teacher.

"Please, we're not making any noise," said Thomas.

"Zzzzzzzzzzz!" said the humbugs, both at once.

"You naughty, disobedient children!" said the teacher angrily. "Be quiet at once!"

"Zzzzzzzzzzz!" said the humbugs, quite enjoying themselves.

"Come out here," said the teacher sternly. Polly and Thomas walked out and stood in the front of the class.

"Now you'll just stay standing out there till you can behave yourselves," said the teacher. "If you hum any more I shall keep you in at playtime."

"Zzzzzzzzzzzzzzzzzzzzzzzz!" went the humbugs, as loudly as ever they could.

The teacher stared at the two red-faced children in surprise. She couldn't think how they dared to disobey like this.

"Is it something you have got in your pockets that is making this noise?" she said suddenly. "Turn out everything you have there, please."

The two children turned out their pockets. Thomas put out a handkerchief, a pocket-knife, a piece of rubber, two bits of string, one marble, a notebook, and the humbug wrapped up in paper. Polly put out a handkerchief, a brown ha'penny, a doll's bonnet, and the humbug wrapped in paper.

Well, as soon as the humbugs found themselves out in the cold air, they stopped humming and were perfectly quiet.

The teacher looked carefully at everything. "Put them back," she said. "I can see nothing there that would make a noise. I see you have both stopped humming now. Go back to your

"ZZZZZZZZZ!" WENT THE HUMBUGS, AS LOUDLY AS
EVER THEY COULD

seats and don't let me hear another word from you for the rest of the morning."

The children went back to their seats. They couldn't understand it. Whatever was making that noise? If they had found bees in their pockets they wouldn't have been at all surprised. But there were no bees there at all.

They began to do their writing. The humbugs got warm again. They began to hum, quite quietly at first, but more loudly as they got nice and warm.

"Zzzzzzzzzzz!" said the one in Thomas's pocket.

"Zzzzzzzzzzz!" sang Polly's humbug gaily. Every one looked up. The teacher frowned and rapped on the desk.

"Polly! Thomas! You have begun to hum again. You will lose your playtime."

"Zzzzz-zzz-zzz-zz!" hummed the two humbugs, sounding quite pleased. "Zzz-zzz-zzz-zzz!"

"Go out of the room," said the teacher. "I won't have you in here, disturbing the class."

Thomas and Polly went out of the room and stood behind the door. How they hoped that the head master wouldn't come along and see them there!

Well, he did! He came walking along, and when he saw the two children standing outside the door with drooping heads he stopped in surprise.

"And what are you standing out here for, instead of working in the classroom?" he asked sternly.

Thomas and Polly opened their mouths to answer, but the humbugs got in first. "ZZZZZZZZZZZZZ!" they hummed, and the head master stared in the greatest astonishment.

"You had better come to my study," he said. The two children followed him, wondering what was going to happen.

"I believe it's those humbugs we took from Dame Quick-Eyes," whispered Thomas to Polly. "I believe they are humming. There must be some magic in them. We'd better throw them away when we get the chance."

But they didn't have a chance, for they were soon in the head master's study. He sat down and looked at the two children sternly.

"Now what is the meaning of this?" he asked.

"Zzz-zzz-zzz-zzz!" went the humbugs gaily. The head master could hardly believe his ears. He was just about to speak very sharply indeed to the children, when some one went by the open window, carrying a basket of washing. It was Dame Quick-eyes, taking back the head master's clean shirts.

Now Dame Quick-Eyes had quick ears as well as eyes, and as soon as she heard that humming sound she quite well what it was. She peeped in at the window.

"Zzzzzzzzzzzzzzzzzz!" went the humbugs cheerfully. Dame Quick-Eyes grinned. She guessed at once that the two children had been to her house and taken her humbugs. When the sweets had begun to hum, the children had got into trouble. Serve them right!

Dame Quick-Eyes called in through the window. "Good morning, Mr. Head Master. I think I can tell you what is making that noise. Look in the children's pockets and you will find some of my hummybugs. It is they that are making that noise!"

It wasn't long before the humbugs were on the master's desk – but, of course, they stopped humming as soon as they were out of the warm pockets.

"Pick one up in your hand and warm it, sir," said Dame Quick-Eyes. The head master did so – and at once the humbug, feeling the warmth there, began to hum cheerfully.

"Zzzzzzzzzzzz!" it sang, "Zzzzzzzzz!"

"Good gracious me!" said the head master, in the greatest surprise. "Where did these come from?"

The children went very red. Polly began to cry. "We t-t-t-took them out of a b-b-b-bag we saw on Dame Quick-Eyes' t-t-t-table this morning!" she sobbed.

"That is stealing," said the master sternly. "I've a good mind to make you keep these humbugs in your pockets for a week or two, so that they may tell every one of your naughty ways."

"Please don't!" begged Thomas and Polly. "We'll never, never do such a thing again "

They didn't. They threw the humbugs away on a rubbish-heap, and there they will stay till some one lights a bonfire and then what a surprise the gardener will get! You know what he'll hear, don't you, as soon as those humbugs get warm. "Zzzzzzzz! Zzzzzzz! Zzzzzzzzzzz!"

# CHAPTER TWENTY-TWO

## *Daddy's best knife*

Daddy was very cross with Dick, because Dick had borrowed his best pocket-knife and had lost it.

"You are a naughty little boy," said Daddy. "First you borrow my knife without asking me – and then you are careless enough to leave it somewhere about the garden. It will get rusty and will be no use at all."

"I've hunted for it everywhere, Daddy," said Dick. "I'm very, very sorry."

"Well, until you find my knife I forbid you to use your best toy," said Daddy. "Then perhaps you will learn not to lose other people's things."

Dick looked very upset. "Oh, Daddy, my new bow and arrows are my best toy," he said. "Can't I play with them?"

"No, you can't," said Daddy. "I'm sorry, Dick, but you really must learn to be careful with things that belong to other people. You'd better hunt for that knife if you want to play with your bow and arrows."

Dick went out to hunt again. Peter, his little brother, went with him. Dick felt sure he had looked in every single place in the garden, but he looked again.

"I had it here, when I was sharpening an arrow," he said, standing by the garden seat. "But the knife isn't here."

"And you had it over there when you sharpened my pencil," said Peter. "But it isn't there either."

"I simply don't know *where* it can be," said Dick gloomily. "It's just disappeared!"

"It's such a shame you can't play with your bow and arrows," said Peter. "We were having such fun, weren't we?"

"Yes," said Dick. "I'll have to put them away, I suppose."

"Daddy didn't say *I* mustn't play with them," said Peter. "Would you let *me* play with them, Dick?"

"No," said Dick. "They are mine."

"Well, couldn't I just have a turn with them?" said Peter, who really did love a bow and arrows.

"No, you can't," said Dick. "I don't want people to play with my things when *I'm* not allowed to."

"Oh, Dick, you might let me!" begged Peter. "I'd be ever so careful. I wouldn't lose a single arrow."

Dick thought about it. He didn't want to let Peter have his bow and arrows at all. It would be horrid to see him playing with it, when he, Dick, was not allowed to.

"I really can't let you," Peter," he said. "You go and play with your train."

"It's broken," said Peter. He turned away, disappointed. Dick saw him looking unhappy, and he put out his hand and pulled him back. He was a kind-hearted boy, and he didn't like to see his brother looking miserable.

"All right, Peter, you can play with my bow and arrows," he said. "I won't mind. But I don't want to see you shooting. It would make me feel horrid. I shall go and read in the play-room whilst you have my bow."

He went off. Peter was pleased to think he could have the toy he wanted, and he danced off to get the beautiful bow and arrows. Soon he was pretending to be a Red Indian and was shooting at enemies all over the place. What fun it was!

When he heard the bell ringing for dinner-time he ran to collect all the arrows. He knew there were twelve of them. He found eleven – but he couldn't seem to find the last one anywhere! Oh dear, what would Dick say if he lost one!

"I wonder if it flew up on the shed?" he thought. So he stood on the garden seat and then climbed on the shed to see. And, sure enough, the arrow was there.

And what do you think was lying beside it? Why, the knife that Dick had lost! Of course! Dick had sat up on the shed whilst he was carving a little boat yesterday. Peter remembered quite well now.

He put the knife in his pocket, scrambled off the shed with the arrow and rushed into the house. "Dick! Dick! One of your arrows found Daddy's knife! Look! It was up on the shed!"

"Oooh! good, good, good!" said Dick, delighted. "Mother, look – here's Daddy's knife found again. Isn't that lucky?"

"Well, Dick, you got it back because you were kind enough to let Peter play with your bow and arrows!" said Mother.

"If you'd been selfish and put them away that arrow would never have found the knife for you. Kindness always comes back to you somehow."

Dick cleaned Daddy's knife for him, and then he and Peter played Red Indians all the afternoon with the bow and arrows. They *did* have a good time, I can tell you!

## CHAPTER TWENTY-THREE

### *Ronnie gets a shock*

Ronnie was a lucky boy – I can't tell you how many toys he had! He had soldiers and trains and motorcars and books and tops and aeroplanes and everything else you can imagine. He *was* lucky.

He was something else besides lucky – he was careless! It didn't matter what time of day you went into Ronnie's play-room, it was always scattered with toys – and Ronnie trod on them as he went to and fro! He threw them into corners when he had finished playing with them. He broke them. He left them out in the rain.

"Really, Ronnie!" his mother said to him, "you don't deserve to have such lovely toys. No sooner are they given to you than you are careless with them and break them or spoil them."

"I don't," said Ronnie sulkily.

"You do, Ronnie," said his mother. "You left that new golliwog out in the rain yesterday and he's a dreadful sight now – and you left your new hammer out too, and it's rusty. You trod on about twenty of your soldiers to-day and broke them. And now I see your lovely new motor-car has a wheel off!"

"I don't care!" said Ronnie.

"Be careful, Ronnie!" said his mother. "You know the old saying, don't you? 'Don't care was *made* to care!' Something may happen to make *you* care!"

"I don't care if it does," said Ronnie.

Now, although Ronnie didn't know it, a little old witch-woman called Mrs. Make-you-Care was passing by the window just then. She couldn't be seen – but she saw Ronnie all right!

She had a kind face, but she could be very stern indeed. She looked in the window and nodded to herself.

"He wants a lesson," she said, "he wants a lesson! I'll see he gets it!"

Now that afternoon Ronnie was to go out to a party at his cousin's. He was most excited. He put on his sailor suit with long trousers. This was his party suit. He looked very nice in it – most grown up!

He went off to the party – and close behind him, quite unseen, was Mrs. Make-you-Care, the little witch-woman! She trotted after him to the party – and do you know, just as Ronnie got to the door she made him ever so much smaller than he really was! He became just about the size of a doll – and in his sailor suit he looked exactly like a sailor doll!

Ronnie was astonished to find everything suddenly looking so big! He didn't know *he* had gone small, you see! He slipped in at the door when it was opened and went upstairs to the nursery, where the children were playing games at the party.

Now when he came into the room the children thought he must be a walking sailor doll that Ronnie's cousin Leslie might have for his birthday that day! A little girl picked him up and waved him about.

"What a fine sailor doll!" she cried. "Isn't he grand!"

And then poor Ronnie knew what had happened! Somehow or other he had been changed into a doll. He had on his sailor suit – he felt just like Ronnie to himself – but he was nothing but a doll to the others!

He didn't have time to think about it much. The children passed him from hand to hand and looked at him carefully. His cousin Leslie was surprised to see him.

"I don't remember any one giving me a sailor doll for my birthday," he said. "Let's not play with him – we'll play nuts and may. That's fun!"

He took hold of poor Ronnie and threw him down into a corner. Bang! Ronnie bumped his head so hard against the wall that the tears came into his eyes. He tried to get up – but he was a proper doll now and couldn't move!

He lay there watching the children playing nuts and may

and musical chairs and all kinds of games. He saw them sitting down to a glorious tea, with jellies and cream-cakes and chocolate blancmange. He couldn't play games – and he couldn't eat the tea. How upset he was!

He didn't like belonging to Cousin Leslie.

"Leslie isn't kind to his toys," thought Ronnie, quite forgetting that it was he who had taught Leslie to throw his toys about and be careless with them: "I shan't like living here. If only I could run away! However did I become a doll? It is most peculiar. I wish I hadn't said 'Don't care' so often now!"

Nobody took any notice of him after tea. The children had a fine time hunting for presents, and after that they went into the next room to see a conjurer doing clever tricks. Ronnie tried to peep round the doorway and see him too, but he couldn't.

Soon the children said good-bye and went home. Cousin Leslie ran into the nursery. He had ten minutes before bed-time. He was tired and excited.

He caught sight of the sailor doll in the corner and picked him up.

"You're a funny sort of doll! he said. "I don't much like your face. I don't think I want to play with you, but I'll just see if you can stand on your head."

He stood Ronnie on his head – but of course Ronnie couldn't do that, and over he fell, bumping his knees hard. "You're a silly doll!" said Leslie. "I'll stand you on your head in the inkpot!"

He opened the lid of the big ink-pot and stuck Ronnie into the pot, so that his legs waved in the air, and his hair was right in the ink!

Leslie laughed and pulled him out. Poor Ronnie! His hair was black with ink and his hat was quite spoilt. Drops of ink ran down his face.

"You look dreadful now," said Leslie and threw him down on the floor. Bump! All the breath was knocked out of Ronnie's body. He lay there and tried to get his breath back.

"What a horrid, horrid boy Leslie is," thought Ronnie, quite forgetting that he had dipped a doll in the pond the day before! He watched Leslie looking at a book.

It wasn't long before Leslie had finished turning over the pages. He got up to get another book. Ronnie was lying on the floor just at his feet. Do you suppose Leslie stepped over

Ronnie or picked him up to put him safely out of the way?

No! He trod right on top of him! Yes – as hard as he could too! Just as Ronnie had always trodden on any of *his* toys if they had been in his way!

Ronnie gave a loud squeal. Leslie looked down in surprise. "Oh, I didn't know you were a doll that could squeak!" he said. And he trod on Ronnie again!

"Ooooooooooh!" said poor Ronnie at once, because he was hurt. Leslie's foot was hard and heavy.

"What a fine noise you make!" said Leslie, and he stamped hard on Ronnie. Poor Ronnie couldn't even squeal then! He had no breath left at all!

"I suppose I've broken your squeak," said Leslie, and he kicked Ronnie hard. Ronnie rose into the air and flew right out of the open window!

Out he went – and into the garden. Flop! He fell on to the grass lawn and lay there blinking. He felt as if he were bruised all over.

Then he heard Leslie's mother calling him to bed. "Oh dear, oh dear!" thought Ronnie. "I do hope Leslie remembers I'm out here on the grass! I don't want to be left out in the dark and the cold."

Of course Leslie didn't remember to go and fetch Ronnie in. He thought Ronnie was just a sailor doll, and he didn't even think about him any more.

And so Ronnie lay out on the grass and watched the night coming. It grew darker and darker. The dew came on the grass and Ronnie felt wet and cold. And then it began to rain!

Ronnie couldn't think what the big stinging drops were that smacked him hard all over his body! They felt so very big now that he was small!

"Oh, my goodness – it must be raining!" he groaned at last. "I shall get all soft and squashy like the golliwog I left out in the rain the other day!"

Ronnie lay still whilst the rain wetted him from head to foot. He began to think about his own toys at home. How they must have hated it when he was so careless with them! How they must have hated him too! And now Leslie had done just the same to him!

"I wish I hadn't said, 'I don't care,' to mother," said Ronnie, out loud. "I was silly. I was horrid. Now I shall never have the chance to show I'm sorry!"

Mrs. Make-you-Care was listening nearby. When she heard what Ronnie said she nodded her head. She went softly over to him and blew down his neck. Ronnie thought it was a little wind. He didn't know it was a bit of magic. He grew back to his own size again – very, very slowly, so that he didn't notice it. He was able to move! He got up and walked about. What should he do next?

"I think I'll try and find my way home," said Ronnie. "Perhaps my mother will know me, even though I'm a doll now."

So, in the rain and the dark he made his way back home. The back door was open. He crept inside. He went up the stairs to find his mother. Everything seemed the right size again – but Ronnie was so tired and wet and cold that he hardly noticed it! He saw his bed standing in the corner, and he threw off his clothes and crept into it.

In two minutes he was fast asleep! And in the morning he woke up sneezing. Oh, what a dreadful cold he had got!

"Ronnie, how in the world did you get that cold?" asked his mother, surprised. "And why is your hair so inky?"

Ronnie knew quite well – but he was much too ashamed to tell! And dear me, I'd just like you to go and see his toys now – you couldn't see a happier lot, not one of them broken or spoilt!

I don't expect he'll say "Don't care!" any more, do you?

CHAPTER TWENTY-FOUR

## The most surprising chair

Once there was a lazy child called Susan. She wouldn't get up in the morning, she wouldn't hurry herself to dress, and even in the daytime she would flop down into an arm-chair and stay there till her mother tipped her out.

She was always late for morning school, and her teacher scolded her hard. But when she began to be late for afternoon school as well, her teacher wondered whatever was the matter.

"Well, you see," explained Susan, "I do feel so sleepy after my dinner that I curl up in an arm-chair and fall asleep. When I wake up I'm late. My mother won't bother about me any more, so I'm afraid I shall always be late!"

Now the arm-chair that Susan curled up in after her dinner was an old, old one. It loved people to sit in it, and it was good to old people and made itself as comfy as possible for them.

But it really couldn't bear lazy people, and when Susan, who was young and strong, curled up in it so lazily every day, the old chair grumbled away to itself and tried to make its seat as hard and as uncomfortable as it could.

But it wasn't a bit of use. Susan didn't even notice it was hard. She went off to sleep at once! She always ate too much at dinner-time and this made her very sleepy.

The chair creaked loudly. Susan didn't wake. The chair made its seat as hard as wood and its arms like iron. Susan didn't stir. The school bell rang loudly. Susan slept peacefully on. And this happened every afternoon. Wasn't it dreadful!

Susan's mother was so tired of scolding her that she no longer bothered to wake her up.

"You can be punished for your lazy ways at school," she said. "I can't be bothered with you any more."

But the old chair grew more and more angry. It worked itself up to such a state that one afternoon a most peculiar thing happened.

Susan had eaten a big plate of meat-pie and had had three helpings of treacle pudding. She felt very sleepy as usual, and curled up in the old chair. She fell asleep and even snored a little.

This was too much for the chair. It gave an angry creak and then another. It shook itself. It lifted up a foot and tapped loudly on the floor

Susan slept on! The chair tapped with another foot. Susan snored gently. Oh, naughty Susan, wake up, before anything happens!

The chair lost its temper.

"I've four feet and four legs. I can walk on them as well as stand on them. I'll take this lazy child to school and see what she says when she wakes up there!"

And with that the chair lifted up first one leg, then another – and soon it was walking out of the room, making a clip-clop noise on the floor as it went.

Susan slept peacefully on. The chair went into the hall. The front door was open, and the postman was just putting a letter on the mat. He saw the chair, gave a frightened shout and rushed off! The chair gave a creak and went out of the front door.

Well, as soon as it was in the street, with people walking near, every one stopped in surprise. They stared at the chair, they nudged one another when they saw the sleeping Susan, and they looked half frightened. But nobody tried to stop the chair until it met Mr. Plod the policeman.

He saw the chair coming towards him and looked most astonished. When it came near him, making a clip-clop noise with its feet on the pavement, he cleared his throat politely – "er-hurrrrr!" – and put up his hand.

"Stop!" he said. But the chair took no notice at all. It just gave a loud and rather rude creak, and went under the policeman's hand. Mr. Plod was annoyed. He took out his notebook and ran after the chair.

"Are you a new kind of motor-car?" he cried. "Where's your licence? You haven't got a number-plate!"

The chair creaked again and set off so fast that the policeman was soon left behind. It bumped into Mrs. Hurry and gave her a dreadful shock. It trod on Mr. Toppy's foot and made him hop about in pain, and he shouted in surprise to see such a curious sight as an arm-chair hurrying by with a little girl fast asleep in it.

At last the arm-chair reached the school. The children had all gone in, but the door was still a little open. The teacher was calling the children's names to see that they were all in time.

"Alice! Ben! Mary! Mollie! Eric!"

"Here, Miss Brown. Here, Miss Brown," answered the children politely, as their names were called.

And then Miss Brown came to Susan's name. "Susan!" she called – and at that very moment the door opened and in came the arm-chair with Susan!

"Look! Look!" shrieked all the children. "Susan's in time – the chair has brought her! She's fast asleep – oh, she's fast asleep!"

They all began to laugh loudly as they gathered round the creaking arm-chair, which was now standing still by Miss Brown's desk.

HE SAW THE CHAIR, GAVE A FRIGHTENED SHOUT
AND RUSHED OFF

Susan awoke, for the noise was really almost deafening. She rubbed her eyes and looked around.

"Oh!" she said. "Where am I? I've been asleep! How did I come to school?"

"The arm-chair brought you, the arm-chair brought you!" shouted the children, dancing round in delight. "It was awake, and it brought you by itself! Oh, what a funny thing, Susan!"

Susan was ashamed. She got out of the arm-chair and ran to her desk. She sat down, very red.

When the chair saw Susan safely at her desk it gave a creak as if to say good-bye, and clip-clopped to the door. It squeezed out and clip-clopped home, taking no notice of any one. Susan had got to school in time for once!

Well, do you know, Susan got teased so much about the chair bringing her to school, and was so afraid that perhaps her bed might play her the same trick in the morning, that she quite turned over a new leaf. Now she is up as soon as her mother calls her, and she never dares to go to sleep after dinner.

So she isn't late for school any more and has got as many good marks as any one. But if the chair sees her yawning, you should hear it creak!

"Cr-eeeeeeeeeak!" it goes. And Susan stops yawning at once and gets some work to do. Poor old Susan! She never sits in that old arm-chair any more, as you can guess!

## CHAPTER TWENTY-FIVE

### *The boy who threw stones*

Once upon a time there was a boy called Sammy. He could throw and catch very well indeed, so he was a good cricketer, and fine at all ball games.

He could throw stones very well too. If you drove a nail lightly into a tree-trunk, Sammy could stand quite a good way off, throw a stone and hit the tiny nail so hard that it was driven into the tree!

Sammy was proud of his throwing. But he didn't only throw stones at marks in trees and things like that – he threw them at birds, cats, and dogs. And because he was such a good shot he always hit them.

The other boys and girls couldn't bear to see birds and animals hurt.

"Please don't throw stones, Sammy," they begged. But Sammy laughed.

"The birds and animals should get out of the way more quickly!" he said, and threw a stone at a cat asleep on a wall. The stone hit her on the back and she woke up with a loud mew of pain.

Now one little girl had a great-grandmother who looked like a kindly old witch, with twinkling eyes and a mouth that was always smiling. Ellie, the little girl, used to visit her Great-Granny every Friday, after school, and she made up her mind to tell her about Sammy.

"Perhaps Great-Granny can stop him from being so unkind," she thought. "I'll ask her."

So, when she was sitting down to a fine tea of bread and honey, chocolate cake and ginger biscuits, Ellie told Great-Granny about Sammy.

"You see, Great-Granny," she said, "he's so proud of being a good shot that he throws stones at all the birds and animals he sees. And oh, Great Granny, he broke a robin's leg the other day. It made me cry to see it."

Great-Granny's mouth looked rather stern.

"A boy who can do that needs a lesson," she said, and her kind eyes stopped twinkling.

"That's what I thought," said Ellie, eating a ginger biscuit and staring at her Great-Granny. "I wondered if *you* knew how to teach him a lesson, Great-Granny. You are so old and wise, aren't you?"

"I might be able to," said Great-Granny. "I will think about it. Now, eat your tea and don't worry any more about Sammy."

So Ellie ate her tea and talked about her tortoise, which was getting sleepy. Ellie thought she ought to put it in a box to sleep for the winter.

All the time that Great-Granny was talking to Ellie about her tortoise she was thinking how she might teach Sammy a lesson. And at last she thought of a way. Then she smiled, and

Ellie wondered what made Great-Granny rub her hands together in glee all of a sudden.

After Ellie had gone, Great-Granny took a sheet of paper and wrote something on it. She pinned it up on the fence outside her front garden, ready for Sammy to see when he came by. Then she went indoors and made a strange mixture which she poured into a lemonade jug.

Now, when Sammy came by that way, it was Saturday morning, and there was no school. He was whistling as he walked, and held in his hand some small stones ready to throw at anything he saw. When he saw the notice outside Ellie's Great-Granny's house, he stopped and read it. This is what it said:

---

TO ALL GOOD THROWERS
A THROWING MATCH
WILL BE HELD AFTER TEA TO-DAY.
WALK IN AND TRY YOUR LUCK

---

"Oooh!" said Sammy. "Good! I'll certainly go in for this throwing match. How lucky I came this way and saw the notice!"

So, after tea that day, with his pocket full of smooth stones, Sammy walked in at Great-Granny's front gate and knocked at her door. She opened it.

"Ah! A thrower!" she said. "Come in, come in!"

Sammy went in. He looked round. Nobody else seemed to be there.

"Will you have a drink of lemonade?" asked Great-Granny, and she poured him out a glass of the strange mixture she had made. Sammy drank it. It was very sweet, and he thought it was nice, but not a bit like lemonade.

"Sit down in this chair," said Great-Granny, and Sammy sat down. He felt very sleepy. He blinked and he blinked. Suddenly he heard another knock at the door. Great-Granny opened it, and to Sammy's enormous surprise, two dogs came in, walking on their hind legs, talking to one another.

Sammy sat up and stared. Could he be dreaming? Before he could make up his mind there came another knock, and this time three cats came in, also walking on their hind legs,

100

chattering away gaily. Then three hens ran in on long legs, and two ducks. Then with a rush, came a crowd of smaller birds – blackbirds, thrushes, sparrows, and robins. One of the robins had its leg bandaged all the way up.

"I can't make this out," said Sammy to Great-Granny, who was busy welcoming every one. "You don't seem surprised to see all these animals and birds coming in like this! But it seems very astonishing to me."

"Oh, it's the throwing match that has brought them," said Great-Granny. "We'll begin in a minute."

"Are these creatures going in for the throwing match as well as me?" asked Sammy, still more surprised.

"Of course," said Great-Granny. "Now then, every one, let's go out and begin."

She opened the back door and every one trooped out. But instead of there being a little back garden there was a field! At one end were piles of little stones. At the other end there was a place marked for the target.

Sammy was more and more surprised. He stared and stared. A large cock began to crow. Every one fell silent.

"Ladies and gentlemen," said the cock in a loud voice, "the match is about to begin. If any one thinks he is the cleverest thrower here, let him step forward and say so."

Sammy at once stepped forward. "I think I must be the cleverest here," he said. "I never miss what I throw at!"

All the animals and birds began to talk at once.

"He's right! He never misses!" cried a big brown dog. "He threw four stones at me one day and hit me with every one!"

"And he threw a stone at me whilst I was singing in a tree, and hit me on the wing," said a big blackbird.

"Well, you should have seen him throw at *me*!" cried a duck. "I was the other side of the farmyard, and he threw a stone and hit me all that distance away! He's a marvellous thrower!"

Sammy went red with pleasure. To think that every one was praising him like this!

"He threw a stone at me and broke my little leg," said a robin, showing his bandaged leg. "I was on the fence at the bottom of his garden and he threw a stone from his bedroom window. Oh, yes, he's a very good shot indeed."

"Well, as he's such a good shot. I don't think we need to ask Sammy to show us what he can do," said Great-Granny.

"He seems never to miss at all. The thing to do is for you each to have a turn, and we will make Sammy the judge. You shall be the target, Sammy, and tell us if any one hits you with all his stones."

"What! Let every one throw at *me*!" said Sammy, hardly believing his ears.

"Why not?" said Great-Granny. "You can tell very easily then who is a good shot and who isn't, can't you? If a stone hits you, you can shout 'Well thrown!' and if it misses you can shout 'Bad shot!' "

"But I shall be hurt!" said Sammy.

"What does that matter?" said Great-Granny. "All these other creatures were hurt when you practised your throwing weren't they? Well, if you practise on them, why shouldn't they practise on you? Come, come, Sammy, do as you would be done by. If you expect the animals and birds to let you throw at *them*, you must also allow them to throw stones at *you*!"

All the creatures hustled Sammy to the post which was to be the target at which they all must throw.

"Now don't you dare to run away," said a big tabby-cat. "If you do, we shall come after you and scratch you and bite you. Don't spoil our throwing match."

Sammy stood by the post, trembling. He was afraid. It was one thing to throw stones at others – but quite a different thing to have stones thrown at *him*! He didn't like it at all.

"Tabby-cat, you take three stones and try first," said the cock. So the tabby picked up three small pebbles and aimed carefully. Ping! The stone flew through the air and hit Sammy smartly on the ankle.

"Oooh! Ow!" yelled Sammy. "Don't!"

"Good shot!" shrieked every one in delight. The tabby cat was delighted. She threw her two other stones, but neither of them hit Sammy. Then it was the turn of the large brown dog. He picked up a pebble and aimed carefully.

Ping! It hit Sammy on the hand. He hopped about, yelling, rubbing first his ankle and then his hand.

"Don't! Don't!" he cried. "I don't like it! It's unkind!"

"Well, it's what *you* did to us!" yelled back every one. The dog threw again. His second stone went wide, but his third one hit Sammy on the knee. How he shouted!

The animals and birds laughed. This was a fine throwing

HE RAN AND HE RAN WITH ALL THE ANIMALS AND
BIRDS AFTER HIM

match! *They* had been Sammy's targets in the past – and now he was theirs! A blackbird took his three stones and aimed carefully.

He was not a good shot and all three of his stones missed. Sammy was so thankful – but it was a different thing when a brown hen ran up and threw. My goodness, she was a good thrower! Her legs were strong with scratching around the farmyard, and she threw hard and straight.

Ping! She got Sammy on his nose. Ping! Another stone hit him on the neck. Ping! The last one hit him sharply on his wrist. Every one clapped and shouted.

"Oh, good shot, hen, good shot!" But Sammy yelled and hopped around, and then made up his mind to beg for mercy.

"Let me off! Let me off!" he begged. "I will never throw stones at anything again. I didn't know it hurt so much."

"You had your fun with us, and now we want ours with you!" shouted back the animals and birds, and they all rushed to take stones at once. That was too much for Sammy. He gave a frightened yell and tore off for home. He ran and he ran, with all the animals and birds after him. He panted and puffed, and was afraid his legs would give way.

At last he saw some one in the distance and he ran towards her as fast as he could. "Save me! Save me!" he begged, flinging his arms round the surprised person. It was Ellie, going for a walk in the fields!

Ellie stared in astonishment. "What do you want me to save you from?" she asked. "There's no one near that I can see."

Sammy turned round and looked. Sure enough, there wasn't a sign of any animal or bird to be seen.

"Oh, Ellie, Ellie, I've had such a dreadful time," said Sammy. "I saw a notice outside your Great-Granny's about a throwing match – and I went in for it – but all the birds and animals began to throw at *me* and I'm bruised all over. Look!"

"Well, Sammy, I'm sorry for you, but after all your leg isn't broken like that poor little robin's was the other day," said Ellie. "It's a funny tale you are telling me. I can hardly believe it is true."

"Well, come and see the notice outside your Great-Granny's house," said Sammy. "Then you'll believe me."

So they went to see it – but there was no notice there at all! "You must have been dreaming, Sammy!" said Ellie – though she felt sure it was really her Great-Granny who had managed to teach Sammy such a lesson.

"Well, dream or no dream, I'm never going to throw stones at any creature again," said Sammy, and he took every stone from his pockets and threw them on the ground.

"Good," said Ellie. "It's worth a few bruises to have learnt something like that, Sammy."

And what about Sammy now? That was last autumn, and Sammy has never thrown another stone at anything. And whenever he passes Ellie's Great-Granny's cottage and sees the old woman there, he is very polite indeed. You never know what a wise old woman like that will do next!

## CHAPTER TWENTY-SIX

### *The bad little boy*

Once there was a bad little boy called Jo. He was so bad that he was always getting into trouble and being smacked and sent to bed.

He always got as dirty as could be as soon as he had clean clothes on. He always tore his coat as soon as his mother had bought him a new one. He never remembered to wash behind his ears, and as for remembering to wipe his feet or say please and thank you, well, he really didn't seem able to!

His mother was quite in despair. "I shall ask your father to deal with you now, Jo," she said. "I can't manage you any more."

Well, Jo's father had one way of dealing with him that Jo didn't like at all. Do you know what it was? He spanked him well with a slipper!

Now Jo grew to hate those slippers of his father's. There they sat, warming by the fire every evening, and Jo knew quite well that if he had been naughty, they were waiting to spank him! So he hated them and wished he could get rid of them.

And one evening he took them away when nobody was looking. He tucked them under his arm, ran upstairs with

105

them and locked them into his cupboard where nobody would find them. Wasn't he a bad little boy?

Well, his father couldn't *think* what had happened to his slippers when he came home that night! Jo's mother scurried here and there looking for them, and Jo himself pretended to hunt too, though all the time the bad little boy was chuckling to himself, knowing that they were safely locked in the cupboard upstairs.

But, dear me, when Jo was in bed that night, a strange thing happened. The slippers wanted to get out of the cupboard! They were cold there, for they were used to warming themselves by the fire when they were not on Jo's Daddy's feet. So they began to stir about in the cupboard, muttering angrily.

"Let us out! We're cold! We're cold!"

Jo sat up and listened. Whatever was that noise? It came from the cupboard. Could he have shut the cat in there by mistake?

"Let us out! Let us out!" cried the two cold slippers.

"Good gracious! Whatever is it?" thought Jo. "Who is it in the cupboard?" he asked aloud.

"Your father's slippers! We're cold! Let us out!"

"Daddy's slippers! But slippers can't talk!" said Jo.

"Of course we can talk. We've got tongues, haven't we!" said the slippers, and they began to bang at the door.

Jo was frightened. If they made a noise like that they would wake his Mummy and Daddy, and they would find the slippers there and be very angry with him. Whatever was he to do?

"Let us out!" shouted the slippers. Bang, bang! "Let us out!" Bang, bang, bang!

Jo slipped out of bed quickly. He unlocked the cupboard door and the slippers flapped out. They hopped into Jo's bed.

"Oh, no, you can't come there," said Jo, getting into his warm bed. He threw the slippers out on to the floor. "I'm not having you in bed with me, you nasty, horrid things!"

"Let's spank him, shall we?" said one slipper to the other. Jo listened in alarm. The slippers jumped on to the bed and cuddled down beside Jo under the sheet, where it was warm. Jo didn't dare to turn them out again. They dug themselves well into him and went to sleep. Poor Jo didn't sleep for a long time, for he was very worried over this strange happening.

106

He always had to make his own bed in the morning, so he left the slippers sleeping peacefully there, and made his bed carefully so that they didn't show. Then he went down to breakfast, not late for once. He was so quiet that his mother wondered if he was ill.

Jo was quiet because he was thinking of some way to get rid of those dreadful slippers. At last he smiled and rubbed his hands. Gardener had a bonfire burning in the garden this week. He would stuff the slippers there after tea and that would be the end of them!

So, after tea, when no one was looking, the bad little boy slipped down to the bonfire with the sleepy slippers. He stuffed them hard into the heart of the bonfire and then skipped back joyfully to the house. That was the end of those annoying slippers!

But, you know, it wasn't! For, in the middle of the night, Jo heard something rapping at the window. He sat up. Then the moon shone into his room, and there, on the window-sill, he could quite clearly see those two slippers.

"Let us in! Let us in!" shouted the slippers angrily. "We won't be left out on the rubbish-heap! Let us in!"

Well, poor Jo simply *had* to let them in, of course, for he was afraid they would wake up the whole house! So he opened the window and in they jumped, smelling strongly of the bonfire, and rather scorched about the toes.

"You're a bad boy," said the slippers. "If that fire hadn't gone out when the rain came, we might have been burnt. Let us come into your warm bed and cuddle down."

Jo had to let them. He tried to leave them as little room as possible, but those slippers dug their toes into him and squeezed him right to the wall. He was very uncomfortable, and how cross he felt when the slippers began to snore!

"Horrid, nasty things!" he thought. "I'll get rid of them to-morrow without fail. I'll drown them in the river!"

So the next day, when he had a chance, Jo took the slippers out of his bed, tucked them under his coat and ran down to the river.

"Where are you going?" squeaked the slippers, frightened.

"To drown you!" said Jo. "Then you won't spank me any more, or creep into my warm bed at night."

"Oh, yes, we will," said the slippers – but they couldn't say

107

a word more because Jo flung them straight into the water – splash! The slippers sank at once, and Jo ran home, whistling with glee. He had got rid of them at last.

But alas for poor Jo! In the middle of the night, as he was dreaming peacefully, there came a tap-tap-tapping at his window once again.

"Let us in, you naughty boy! Let us in!" cried the voices of the two slippers.

Jo sat up and groaned. "Go away," he said. "I thought I'd drowned you."

"Well, you didn't," said the slippers. "We just walked over the bottom of the river and crept out. But we are very wet and cold, and we want to get into your bed."

Jo was full of horror – what, have those wet slippers in his nice, dry, warm bed! Never!

So he lay down again and tried to go to sleep. But the slippers tap-tapped at the window till Jo thought they would break it.

"We'll go and tap at your father's window," said the slippers. "Yes, we will! And we'll tell him what you have done to his favourite slippers these last two days."

Jo got up. It was no use, he must let those slippers in. So he opened the window and in they came. My goodness, they *were* wet! They made puddles on the carpet as they hopped over to the bed. They jumped in under the sheet and snuggled down warmly.

"This is fine," they said sleepily. "This is just what we want. We were afraid of getting a chill."

Jo got into bed too. The slippers pressed close to him, and his pyjamas got wet and cold. He squeezed himself against the wall – but the slippers came after him and cuddled him close. Jo could not bear it. He felt so wet and cold.

He got out of bed, shivering. He put on his dressing-gown, took the eider-down, wrapped it round him, and tried to go to sleep in the chair. But it was very difficult.

The next day Jo looked white and tired.

"Dear me, Jo!" said his mother, quite worried, "You look as if you are going to have a cold. You had better stay away from school and have a nice lazy day in bed."

Now usually this would have pleased Jo very much, for he was lazy. But to-day he thought of those awful wet slippers in his bed and he didn't want to stay at home at all.

"Oh, I'm quite all right, Mummy," he said quickly. "I don't feel at all like going to bed."

His father was pleased. He looked up from his paper. "Good boy!" he said. "I like to see a boy wanting to go to school instead of lazing in bed."

Jo was pleased. It wasn't often his father found anything to praise, for Jo was usually such a bad little boy. It was nice to find some one talking kindly to him after the way those horrid slippers spoke. He went off to school feeling a bit happier.

What was he to do with those slippers? It wasn't a bit of use trying to get rid of them, for they would only come back in the middle of the night and want to get into his nice warm bed. And Jo had quite made up his mind that he was NOT going to sleep with them any more.

"But what am I to do?" thought the little boy. "I really don't know. I don't want those slippers living with me all my life. How I wish I hadn't taken them!"

Then a thought came into his head. Suppose he told his father what had happened? No – that wouldn't do. His father would never, never believe that slippers could talk or walk by themselves.

"Well, suppose, I put the slippers back in their place by the fire?" thought Jo. "I could say I had found them upstairs. If only Mummy and Daddy would believe me I'd tell them all about the slippers, but they wouldn't. I know what I'll do. I'll tell Daddy honestly that I hid them because I didn't want to be spanked. Then, if he is angry and spanks me, I must put up with it. It will be better than having to sleep with those unkind slippers, anyhow."

So he went to fetch the slippers. They were in his bed, awake, sneezing a little now and again because they had caught a cold in the river.

"Where are you taking us now?" they cried.

"I'm going to put you downstairs by the fire," said Jo firmly. "And I'm going to tell my Daddy how I hid you."

"Oooh!" said the slippers. "Fancy you daring to do that! Well, we shall like to go back there again. It's nice and warm by the fire. And if we get a bit cold at any time we can always warm ourselves up by spanking you when you do anything bad."

"If you think I'm going to let you spank me again you're mistaken!" said Jo. "If I have to be good for the rest of my life, I will – but you are never, never going to spank me again, you nasty, horrid pair of slippers!"

He took them downstairs and put them by the fire. How surprised Daddy was to see them again! Jo went red and spoke up.

"Daddy, I hated those slippers because they spanked so hard, so I took them and hid them. But now I'm sorry I did so. I've brought them back for you. Please forgive me."

"Well, Jo, it was brave and good of you to own up," said Daddy, surprised. "I certainly shan't spank you. I'm proud of you for telling me. Good boy!"

Jo was happy. It was nice to be in his father's good books. He made a face at the slippers. One of them sneezed.

"Oh, Jo, was that you sneezing?" said his mother anxiously. "I hope you're not getting a cold."

"Sounds as if the sneeze came from my slippers, dear," said Daddy, laughing. "But that couldn't be of course. I expect it was the cat."

Well, you'll be glad to know that those slippers have never spanked Jo again. He made up his mind to be good and he was, though his father and mother could never understand what changed him. As for those slippers, they are getting old but they still warm themselves by the fire. And if Jo makes a face at them now and again, I really don't blame him, do you?

CHAPTER TWENTY-SEVEN

## The tell-tale bird

There was once a little girl called Tilly, who told tales all day long. I don't like tell-tales, do you? Well, nobody liked Tilly!

"Mummy, Peter pushed me to-day! Mummy, Ann dirtied her frock! Mummy, Pussy has been lying on your best cushion! Mummy, the postman dropped one of your letters in the mud and dirtied it – I saw him!"

That was how Tilly told tales all the day, and people got so cross with her! Ah, but wait! She didn't know the tell-tale bird was about!

It came one day and flew in at Tilly's window as she brushed her hair before breakfast. It was a blue and yellow bird with rather a long tail. And it looked very queer because it had ears! No bird has ears like those that animals have, but this bird had feathery ones on each side of its head.

"Shoo!" said Tilly, waving her brush at the bird. "Shoo! Go away! Birds are not allowed in the house."

"I am!" squawked the bird in a loud voice. "I am! I'm the tell-tale bird, I am! And I've been looking for a little girl like you for a long time! Yes, a long, long time! I've come to live with you. We ought to be friends, Tilly, for you're a tell-tale girl and I'm a tell-tale bird."

Tilly didn't know what to make of it at all. She decided to tell her mother about the bird when she went downstairs. So down she went – and the bird flew on to her shoulder as she went.

"Mummy, Mummy, this horrid bird flew in at my window!" said Tilly, in her usual grumbling voice.

"Tilly didn't brush her hair properly, Tilly didn't brush her hair properly!" squawked the bird, jumping up and down on Tilly's shoulder in a most annoying way.

"Why, it's a tell-tale bird!" said Mummy, in surprise. "I didn't think there were any left nowadays. Well, Tilly, you'll have to put up with it, I'm afraid, for as long as you tell tales the bird will want to stay with you and be friends."

Tilly pushed it off her shoulder angrily. "Nasty thing!" she said. "Get away! I won't have you here."

The bird flew to the electric light and swung there on the cord.

"Tilly's got dirty nails!" he squawked. "Tilly's got dirty nails "

Tilly was sent to scrub her nails. The bird went with her. The little girl banged the door and wouldn't let the bird come in. But it flew down the stairs, out of the door, and in at the bedroom window. So Tilly had to put up with it.

They went downstairs again together, the bird on Tilly's shoulder. It dug its claws in if Tilly tried to push it off, so she decided it had better stay. But she didn't mean it to come to school with her. Oh dear, no!

They had breakfast. The tell-tale bird had very bad manners

and often snatched at something that Tilly was just going to put into her mouth. It made her jump too, whenever it gave a loud squawk, which it always seemed to be doing.

"Tilly's spilt her milk!" squawked the bird, in delight, when it saw Tilly spill a tiny little drop. "Dirty girl! She's a dirty girl!"

"You horrid tell-tale!" said Tilly, nearly in tears.

"Tilly's hidden her crust under her plate!" squawked the bird in a little while. "She's a naughty girl!"

"It's only because I've got two teeth loose and I can't chew properly!" cried Tilly, in a rage.

"Well, say so then," said her daddy. "Don't hide things and hope we won't notice. That is not at all a brave thing to do."

"Tilly's a coward, a coward, a coward!" screamed the bird joyously. Tilly got up from the table in tears, and said she was going to get ready for school. The bird went with her. As soon as they were upstairs, Tilly got hold of the bird, smacked it hard, and pushed it into her toy-cupboard. She locked the door, got her hat, and tore off to school without even kissing Mummy good-bye. That shows how upset she was!

She was so glad to be rid of the horrid tell-tale bird. She took her place in her class and opened her books. It was sums. She peeped over at the next child's book.

"Billy's got a sum down all wrong, Miss Brown," she said. "He's copied it out wrong."

There was a squawk at the window. There sat the tell-tale bird, its ears cocked up at each side of its head! It had made such a noise in the toy cupboard that Mummy had had to let it out – and it had flown joyfully off to school. As soon as it got there and heard Tilly telling tales as usual, it knew it had found the right little girl.

"Tilly's got a hole in her stocking!" squawked the bird, jigging up and down in delight. "I saw it this morning. And she had to be sent back at breakfast-time to brush her hair again and scrub her dirty nails!"

Tilly went red. The other children giggled. "Good gracious!" said Miss Brown. "A tell-tale bird! I haven't seen one for a very long time. Does it belong to you, Tilly?"

"No," said Tilly, in a rude voice.

"Oh, I do, I do!" cried the bird, flying to Tilly's shoulder and nuzzling its head against her cheek. "I'm Tilly's tell-tale bird! She's a lovely tell-tale! I love her, I do!"

"TILLY'S GOT A HOLE IN HER STOCKING!"
SQUAWKED THE BIRD

"Well, do you mind sitting on the mantelpiece for a bit?" asked Miss Brown. "I really don't think Tilly can work properly with you on her shoulder."

"Oh, with pleasure!" cried the bird, and it flew to the mantelpiece, where it looked in a kindly manner at every one in the class. It was really a most extraordinary bird.

The class worked hard. Suddenly the little boy beside Tilly whispered to the little girl on his other side. At once Tilly put up her hand.

"Miss Brown, Billy's talking and you said we weren't to!" she said.

Miss Brown was just going to say, "Don't tell tales!" when the tell-tale bird gave a tremendously loud squawk and cried:

"Tilly's got ink on her fingers! Tilly's got ink on her fingers! Dirty girl! Dirty girl!"

"Be quiet, you horrid creature!" cried Tilly, trying to rub the ink off her fingers.

"Well, Tilly, you can't blame the bird for doing what you do all day long," said Miss Brown. "You tell tales – and the bird does too! It is only doing what you do."

Nothing more happened till the children went out to play. The bird went to sleep with its head under its wing. Tilly was glad. The children went out into the garden and the bird woke up and went too. Soon Tilly came running in.

"Miss Brown, Miss Brown, Tommy pushed Eileen over! And Dick pulled my hair! And Alice dropped her cake on the ground and then picked it up and ate the dirty pieces –"

The tell-tale bird flew on to Tilly's shoulder and flapped its wings in her face.

"Miss Brown, Miss Brown!" it cried, in a voice very like Tilly's. "Tilly pushed Leslie! And she trod on George's toe on purpose – I saw her! And she fell down and dirtied her clean dress!"

"Dear me!" said Miss Brown. "Well, Tilly, if I listen to your tales, I must listen to the bird's too."

"You're not to listen to the horrid tales the bird tells!" cried Tilly, and she rushed out, crying. She made up her mind not to tell a single tale more that morning. The funny thing is that she didn't! The bird went to sleep again, its head under its wing. School was very happy and peaceful.

Tilly ran home, leaving the bird fast asleep on the mantel-

114

piece. Nobody seemed to remember it, not even Miss Brown. Tilly was pleased. She washed her hands, brushed her hair, and sat down at the dinner-table.

"Well, did you have a nice morning, Tilly!" asked Mummy.

"Yes," said Tilly. "But a lot of the children were naughty, Mummy. Billy copied his sum wrong – and Alice got her spelling wrong – and . . ."

The tell-tale bird suddenly flew in at the window with such a loud squawk that Tilly dropped her spoon in fright.

"Here we are again!" said the bird, cocking its feathery ears up straight. "Tilly fell down and dirtied her dress at playtime! Tilly got ink on her fingers! Tilly told tales! Tilly . . ."

"Be quiet!" shouted Tilly, and she threw her spoon at the bird. It caught it neatly in its beak, and then flew to the table. It dipped the spoon into Tilly's plate of meat, potato, and gravy and began to eat solemnly. Tilly was so angry.

"Now listen, Tilly," said her mother. "You will have to put up with the tell-tale bird. It only comes to people who tell tales, and it is your own fault that it has come to you. Stop telling tales, and the bird will soon go somewhere else!"

"I'll never tell another tale in my life!" wept Tilly.

But although she had made up her mind about this, she found it was much more difficult than she had thought. She was such a dreadful little tell-tale that it was very difficult for her to stop suddenly.

Whenever she forgot and told a tale, the tell-tale bird was delighted and at once shouted out a whole lot of things about Tilly!

"Tilly lost her hair-ribbon yesterday! Tilly got smacked this morning for being rude! Tilly had to stay in at school for getting her sums wrong! Tilly broke a cup at tea-time! Tilly's a baby, she spilt her cocoa down her front!"

So the bird went on, and there was no way of stopping it at all, except by Tilly never telling a tale herself. In about a month Tilly had stopped telling tales. She always thought twice before she spoke now, and became a much nicer little girl. The other children began to like her. She was asked out to tea and made a lot of friends.

And one day the tell-tale bird flew away! It squawked for the last time on the mantelpiece.

"You're no good at telling tales now, Tilly! I'm going to look for some one else! It's no fun here now!" And it spread its blue-and-yellow wings, flew out of the window and disappeared.

I'm not quite sure where it went to – but if you hear people say, "Ah, a little bird told me!" you may be sure that tell-tale bird is somewhere about, telling tales and secrets just as it did when it was with Tilly!

## CHAPTER TWENTY-EIGHT

### *He forgot his ears!*

Once upon a time there was a little boy called Pip. His real name was Philip but they called him Pip for short.

He was a good boy and a jolly boy – but oh, how he DID hate washing! It was a most peculiar thing but no sooner had he washed his hands than they seemed dirty again – and as for his face, it always seemed to have a smudge on it. Poor Pip!

But what he got into most trouble about was washing behind his ears. Every single day his mother scolded him because he forgot.

"Pip, you haven't washed *behind* your ears," she would say. "Go back to the bathroom at once and wash all round and behind them. Good gracious, there is enough dirt there to grow potatoes!"

So back to the bathroom Pip would have to go and would rub and scrub behind his ears till he was quite clean.

But every morning he forgot again, and in the end his mother got very cross.

"I do wish I hadn't got to tell you *every* morning, Pip!" she said. "Why can't you remember without being told? You wash in front of yours ears – why can't you wash behind too?"

One day Pip's mother went away to stay with Pip's Granny, and Pip was left at home with Ellen the maid. Now Ellen was too busy to bother about how Pip washed himself. So long as his hands were clean she didn't look behind his ears. So you can guess that Pip didn't wash them at all. And my goodness me, they soon needed it!

Pip went to school each day with other boys and girls. And do you know, after his mother had been away a week, a most extraordinary thing happened!

Pip was sitting at the front of the class, and every one was doing handwork. The children were allowed to talk to one another then, and they loved that lesson. Suddenly the little girl behind Pip began to stare and stare and stare at him. Pip felt her staring and turned round.

"Why are you staring at me?" he said.

"Well, what have you got behind your ears?" asked Mary, the little girl, trying to see.

"Nothing, silly, except hair," said Pip.

"I can see something green there," said Mary. "You feel and see."

Pip felt – and what a shock he got! There certainly *was* something growing behind his ears – and it wasn't hair! It felt like stalks!

Mary told the boy next to her, and he stared at Pip too. "It looks as if you've got a plant growing behind your ears," said George. "Did you put it behind there for fun?"

Pip didn't answer. He simply couldn't *imagine* what it was. Just then the bell rang and it was the end of school. The children put away their handwork and went to get their hats. Pip got his first and ran off before the others were ready.

He rushed home. He went to the bathroom and looked in the looking-glass there. And do you know what had happened?

Potatoes were growing behind his ears!

"It's just what Mother said would happen!" groaned poor Pip. "I've been forgetting to wash behind my ears all this week – and I suppose there was enough dirt to grow potatoes! Oh dear, whatever am I to do?"

Really, he did look funny! A potato plant was growing neatly behind each of his ears, sending up nice green stalks with leaves just ready to unfold.

"In a day or two the leaves will open and there will be flowers next!" said Pip. "How every one will laugh at me! I wonder if I can pull up the plants – will it hurt me?"

He tried – and it did hurt him! But he managed to get the roots up at last. Then he pulled the other potato plant from behind his second ear. He threw them into the waste-paper basket.

"Now I'll wash my ears well," he thought. "I simply WON'T

have potatoes growing there. Whatever would Mother say if she saw them! My goodness, it's a good thing Mary saw them this morning. I mightn't have noticed till they were ever so big, and then how every one would have laughed at me!"

He washed his ears so well that they looked as red as tomatoes. Pip was sure they had never been so clean before.

When he went to school that afternoon he found Mary and George waiting for him, with every one else looking excited.

"We told all the children that you were growing potatoes behind your ears," said George, "and they want to see them. And we want to know if you have to water them, and what you do to get the potatoes when they are ready."

"I haven't *got* any potatoes," said Pip, going red. The children went round him and peeped behind his ears.

"Oh, he hasn't any potatoes growing!" they cried in disappointment. "Oh, we did so want to see them!"

The school bell rang. Every one went in. Pip felt that the boys and girls were keeping a watch on him to see if potatoes began to grow suddenly again. He did feel uncomfortable. He kept feeling to see if anything was growing – but it wasn't!

Do you know, Pip washed behind his ears at least six times a day until his mother came home. She *was* surprised to see him looking so clean!

"Whatever has changed you, Pip!" she cried.

"Oh, Mother, I grew potatoes behind my ears one day, just as you said I would," said Pip. "It was dreadful!"

But I really don't think his mother believed him. Do be careful of *your* ears, won't you!

### CHAPTER TWENTY-NINE

## He didn't think

"Mother, I do think you might let me go and do your shopping sometimes," said Peter. "I do really. It would be fun. All the other children do shopping in the town sometimes!"

"I *would* let you, Peter, if only you could be trusted to look where you are going, when you cross the roads," said his mother. "But you never think of looking left and right. You don't even stop when you get to the kerb! I am always afraid you will be knocked down."

"Well, let me take Jock with me," said Peter. Jock was his dog. Peter loved him with all his heart, and thought he was the best dog in the world. "You always say I'm safe with him!"

"I certainly think Jock is a very sensible dog!" said Peter's mother. "He's not a bit silly in traffic as most dogs are. *He* stops at the kerb and looks, first right then left, before he crosses. I only wish you were as sensible!"

"I will, Mother, really, I will!" said Peter. "Just try me!"

"Well – I suppose you'll have to be trusted sooner or later!" said Mother. "You can go down to the town to-morrow for the groceries. You can take the big basket with you."

"Jock can carry it to the shops, when it's empty, and I will carry it back when it's full!" said Peter. He felt rather happy and important. After all, he was seven now. He ought to be allowed to go errands!

So the next day he took the big basket out of the cupboard and whistled for Jock. The big dog came bounding up. Peter gave him the basket. Jock took the handle in his mouth. Then the two of them set off.

"Now be careful, Peter!" called his mother.

"Of course, Mother!" said Peter. Down the hill he went, and into the town. He came to the first crossing and had to stop because two or three people were there, waiting to cross too. Peter crossed with them. Jock crossed too, still carrying the basket. Every one smiled to see him. He looked down his nose at the other dogs. Not one of them carried a shopping basket. Jock felt as important as Peter did.

"Hie, Peter! Where are you going?" called Anna from the other side of the road.

"Shopping," said Peter. "Can't stop to play this morning, Anna. Good-bye!"

"Peter! Look out for Bobby. He's got a new tricycle!" cried Anna. "It's a fine one. He might give you a ride."

So Peter looked out for Bobby, and soon he saw him. He was on the opposite side of the road, and he was on his new tricycle. It was a fine one, painted blue and silver.

"Peter! Come and see my new tricycle!" cried Bobby. And, without thinking at all, Peter at once stepped straight off the kerb and into the road!

He didn't look to the right. He didn't look to the left. He only looked at that fine new tricycle.

Jock saw his little master stepping into the road and he ran to the kerb too. But Jock knew that he must stop and look before he crossed the road. Peter's father had taught him that when he was a puppy! So Jock stood for a moment, basket in mouth! and looked quickly up the road.

A lorry was coming, a big one, loaded with a great stack of wood! Jock knew there would not be time to cross over – but Peter was already in the road! Peter would be knocked down. There was no time for him to cross, and he did not even see the lorry! Jock dropped the basket and gave a loud bark.

Peter took no notice, and Jock knew there was only one thing to do. He must spring into the road, almost under the coming lorry, and knock Peter out of danger So the big dog leaped off the kerb, sprang on to the little boy, and sent him spinning to the other side, where he fell with a bump. The lorry missed him by an inch, and the lorry-driver tried his best to swerve away from the dog.

But poor Jock could not get out of the way in time. One of the wheels ran over his back leg. The dog gave a yelp of pain, and lay still in the road, unable to get up. Peter got up and saw what had happened.

In a trice there was a crowd round. "The brave dog!" said somebody. "He pushed the boy out of danger. Silly child – he ran straight out and never even looked to see if anything was coming. But the dog looked."

Peter was by Jock, crying as if his heart would break. "Jock! Oh, Jock! Are you hurt? Oh, your poor, poor leg! Oh, Jock, you saved me, but you got hurt yourself! Why didn't I look as Mother told me to!"

Jock was taken to the animal doctor, and his poor broken leg was set and put into a splint. Peter had to carry him home, crying tears down his cheeks all the way. Jock licked them up as they fell on to his nose. He whined a little.

"Don't be so upset, little master!" he tried to say. "You're only a little boy who hasn't learnt to think properly yet. I'm a big dog, and I know I must look after you."

Peter understood, but it didn't make him feel any better. "I wouldn't be so unhappy if I had hurt myself through my own silliness," he said. "But because I didn't think, *you* are hurt, Jock. And maybe you will never be able to run again!"

**THE BIG DOG LEAPT OFF THE KERB**

Well, Jock *can* run, but he runs with a limp. And whenever Peter sees the limp he is sad. You may be sure he thinks now, when he crosses the road – but wasn't it a pity that poor Jock had to be hurt, before Peter learnt to be sensible!

## CHAPTER THIRTY

## The boy who put out his tongue

William was quite a nice boy, but he had one very silly habit. He *would* put out his tongue at people when he was cross or disagreeable!

Now this, as you know, is a rude thing to do, and people didn't like it.

"It spoils William when he puts out his tongue at me," said Auntie Hilda.

"I'd give that boy of yours a smacking if he were mine, putting out his tongue at me like that!" roared Uncle Harry.

"Doesn't William look ugly and horrid when he puts out his tongue at us?" said all the school children to one another.

His mother was very upset about it, especially when William actually put out his tongue at *her*. She could hardly believe that her own boy would be so bad-mannered and rude.

That afternoon she went to see William's old nurse, who lived in a cottage at the other end of the village. The old nurse had been William's mother's nurse too, so she was very old indeed. When William's mother told her about her little boy's habit of putting out his tongue at people and making every one feel cross, the nurse nodded her head.

"Ah, yes!" she said. "I know a way of curing that! Just send him down to me to-morrow, will you? And don't worry if he doesn't come back for a while. He will be quite safe."

So the next day William's mother sent him to see his old nurse. He was fond of her, and he gave her a hug when he saw her.

"Keep your coat on, William," she said. "I just want you to take a walk into the next village for me, and buy me an ounce of red wool."

So William started off to go to the next village. But some-how the way seemed rather different from any way he had been before. The people he met seemed rather queer, too – they were dressed in bright gay colours, and their ears seemed very long and pointed.

"Almost as if they were fairy folk," said William to himself. He walked along and came to the village. The houses were small and higgledy-piggledy, and the wool shop was very queer indeed, not a bit like William remembered it. The door-way was so low that he had to bend down to get through it, and the shop was very dark.

"An ounce of red wool, please," he said to the old lady in the shop.

She measured out an ounce, wrapped it up, and gave it to William. He went out again, but the old lady called after him. "Come back and shut the door, little boy."

William went back; but before he shut the door he popped his head into the shop and put his red tongue out at the old lady. Wasn't it rude of him?

The old lady jumped up and ran to him. "Dear, dear," she said, taking him by the shoulders, "so your tongue needs seeing to, does it? Put it out again, little boy. Yes, yes, it is not a nice tongue. You need a dose of medicine."

Still holding William very firmly, she took him to a cup-board. From it she took a big bottle of yellow medicine and poured out a tablespoonful. Then, before William knew what was happening the spoon was in his mouth and the horrid, horrid medicine was trickling down his throat.

"Oooh! Ah!" spluttered poor William. "Don't do that."

"It will do you good," said the old lady, patting him on the back. "I'm glad you showed me your tongue just now. I could see you needed a dose of medicine."

William ran angrily out of the shop. He would dearly have loved to put out his tongue at the old lady again, but he didn't dare to now. He ran down the street.

As he went round the corner, he bumped into some one. It was a little round man with big pointed ears and a tall hat on his head. The hat went spinning into the gutter.

"Now, now, boy," said the man angrily. "Pick up my hat, and next time you turn a corner, look where you are going."

William picked up the hat; but as he gave it back he put out his tongue at the angry man. In a trice the man caught hold of him and said, "Dear, dear! Your tongue looks dreadful. Come along home with me and I'll do something about it."

It was no good William struggling. He had to go with the man. He turned in at a gate on which was a big brass plate that said "Dr. Makemwell." So the little round man was a doctor. Oooh!

Dr. Makemwell took William upstairs and made him get undressed. He popped him into bed and fetched a large bottle of red medicine. He pulled down the blinds and then he spoke to William.

"I'm so glad you showed me your tongue," he said. "I could see that you were not at all well, by looking at your tongue. It is quite yellow. Now you must stay in bed all to-day with the blinds down. You must not read or play. It would be best if you didn't have anything to eat, but, if you feel thirsty, drink a little of that medicine by you."

The doctor went out of the room, and William heard the door being locked. He sat up in a fright. Was he really ill? Could the doctor and the old woman really tell by his tongue whether he was ill or not? Whatever was he to do? He was hungry already, and he couldn't bear the thought of staying in bed all day with nothing to eat. As for that horrid-looking medicine, he wouldn't drink a single drop of it. Not he.

The door was locked, for William tried it. He sat on the bed and wondered what to do. Why did he put out his tongue in that silly way? It had got him into this stupid trouble!

He wondered if the window was open. He went across to see. Yes, it was! Below the window was a sloping roof. If William got out on to that, he could slide down the roof to the gutter, and then jump to the ground. He dressed quickly, hoping that the doctor wouldn't come back. He crept out of the window on to the roof outside. He slid down it quietly. It was a big jump to the ground, but William managed it. Once on the ground, he shot away down the garden to the gate, and out he went, free again!

"I'm jolly well going back home now!" thought William to himself. "I don't like this village at all. It's not a bit like it was last time I was here."

He ran down the street. On the other side of the road were some children, all with pointed ears and merry faces. They waved to William.

Did William wave back? No, he did not. He put out his

HE POPPED HIS HEAD IN AT THE DOOR AND PUT OUT
HIS TONGUE AT THE OLD LADY

tongue at them. You might think he would remember not to do that, but, you see, it was such a habit with him.

The children stared in surprise; then they all ran after him and caught him.

"He's ill, he's ill!" they cried. "Did you see him put out his tongue to show us? Come, little boy, we have some pills to make you better."

"I'm not ill," said William. "I'm quite all right, and I don't want any pills."

"But your tongue is bright yellow," cried the children. "Look!"

They stopped William by a mirror in a shop window and he looked at his tongue. The children were quite right – it was bright yellow.

"It must have been that yellow medicine the old lady in the wool shop gave me," he said. But the children would not believe that. They took him to their schoolroom, which was not far off, and called to a thin, tall lady who wore spectacles and was writing something on the blackboard.

"Teacher, teacher!" they cried. "Here is a boy with a yellow tongue. He put it out to show us how bad it was. Give him some of your pills."

"Dear, dear!" said the teacher, and she went to a cupboard. She took out a box of pills and emptied three into her hand. "Show me your tongue," she said to William; and as soon as he put it out she popped the three pills into his mouth, held his nose till he swallowed them, and then beamed at him.

"I hope you didn't taste them much," she said. "I know they are very horrid."

"Ooooh!" said poor William, for the pills were just about the horridest he had ever tasted. "Oooh! Give me a drink of water, please. I can't bear this horrid taste in my mouth."

The teacher gave him a drink of water. The children went out to play. William felt that he simply couldn't bear this village any longer – what with horrid medicine, and being locked up in a bedroom and then dreadful pills – really, it was terrible! He slipped out of the door and down the street again.

A man on a bicycle nearly knocked him over. But do you suppose William put out his tongue at him? No, he did not! He wasn't going to have any more pills or medicine.

A butcher-boy passed him, whistling loudly. Did William

put out his tongue? No, he certainly didn't. He kept it firmly in his mouth, you may be sure, and ran on down the road.

He ran and he ran; and at last he came back to his own village, and there was the cottage of his old nurse. How glad he was to see it! He ran in and gave the old lady a hug.

"Here's your wool," he said.

"You've been a long, long time, William," said the old lady.

William went red. He wasn't going to tell his old nurse all the things that had happened to him! He knew she would laugh.

But there was such a twinkle in her eyes that William couldn't help feeling she knew something. He said good-bye and went home.

He looked at his tongue in the looking-glass. It was still bright yellow. How dreadful! He must be careful not to let any one see it – people seemed to be so silly about tongues.

So William kept his tongue to himself, and every one was surprised to find that he no longer put it out when he felt cross or cheeky.

It isn't yellow now – it gradually got right again. That was lucky for William, wasn't it?

# MARVELLOUS ENID BLYTON

Enid Blyton could turn her hand to almost any form of writing. Did you know that for a long time she was the contributor on English fauna for the renowned Encyclopaedia Britannica? She wrote plays which were produced all over the world, poetry and hundreds of long and short stories.

In the Dragon series we have her two most celebrated stories about schools – Malory Towers and St. Clare's books, six volumes in each. Many children are so captivated by these stories, believing them to be based on fact, that they write in to us asking us how they can become pupils at these delightful schools. We have to inform them, regretfully, that Malory Towers and St. Clare's have no existence outside the imagination of their author.

Also in the Dragon series are the exciting "Mystery" stories, concerning the Five Find-Outers (and Buster the dog), not forgetting young 'Ern and Mr. Goon the village policeman. Thrilling stories – they have been read and enjoyed by millions of children around the world. If you haven't read them all, decide you are going to collect every one!

You should start your own Dragon library – a Dragon a week, and in such a short time you would have a collection of books to be proud of, gay in colour, bringing brightness to your room, and always there to bring you the pleasure of re-reading your old favourites. Why not determine to buy a Dragon book every week? They are still the finest value on the market.